Babes In Adland

Monica De Vargas

**The New
Atlantian Library**

ABSOLUTELY AMAZING eBOOKS

Published by Whiz Bang LLC, 926 Truman Avenue, Key West, Florida 33040, USA.

For information contact:
Publisher@AbsolutelyAmazingEbooks.com
ISBN-13: 978-1945772047 (The New Atlantian Library)
ISBN-10: 1945772042

Babes In Adland

Table of Contents

Prelude

These pages are dedicated to the Women of Advertising. Those fierce and fearless individuals who, no matter what age, experience, race, sexual orientation, political background or religious bent, are known to me to be smart, hardworking and talented, and are, all too often, driven to make it in a world that promises the moon and delivers, time and time again, only the faintest of starlight.

Here's to those playful, powerful, persistent and praiseworthy women who really do have the courage of their feminine convictions.

Babes one and all, now and forever...

Chapter 1

WELCOME TO ADLAND

For your listening pleasure: *"Girls Just Want to Have Fun" - Cyndi Lauper*

Quote for the day: *"It's amazing how far a good blowjob can take you in this place."*

No matter how often I heard that phrase, it was just as potent (forgive the pun) as the first time I overheard a co-worker say it to one of the new recruits. And it was so true. In a world where appearance is more honored than substance, the right look or the right sexual conquest was just as useful as your college degree – perhaps more so in the wacky, wonderful, wicked world known as Adland. You know, like Tomorrowland, or Fantasyland, or even Frontierland (with all due respect to Mr. Disney,) where dreams really do come true and all barriers are broken down the moment a man's pants drop to his knees waiting for that first tender touch of some new assistant's candy-coated, glossed and glistening lips, waiting to show just how far they are willing to go to get to the top of the heap. To have a chance at the next new account, or the next big campaign, or the next promotion; up the ladder to your own job, if that's where it leads.

There is no shame in this, so don't get me wrong. I hold no judgment whatsoever at the plays made by a young go-getter, hell-bent on making a career in the business of informing and persuading the buying public to use a particular product or service, since that's the sole purpose of an ad. As one ad guru said early on, "It's only creative if it sells." But the measure of how creative something is here at Hamilton, Ingersoll & Pride, Inc., (hereafter referred to as HIP, Inc.,) might well be in direct proportion to the volume of some executive's climax, and how fast the news of it spreads along the agency grapevine, which, as everyone here knows, is much more efficient than anything AT&T has to offer.

Permit me to share some background info. I began doing my time in the ad game in the late '70s, when "sex, drugs, and rock 'n roll" left their mark on every aspect of your life, from fashion to music, to how people danced, and talked, and screwed, and the very word S-E-X was not exactly a dirty word, unless the advertiser was *Procter and Gamble*, or *Warner-Lambert*, or *Sears Roebuck & Co.*, where home, mother, family and country were better words. However, if you were *Ford*, or *Smirnoff*, or *Phillip Morris*, there was no limit to how far you could push it in an ad, until the issues of highway safety and the price of pollution, the threat of cancer and the sorrows of addiction eventually came to the forefront as negative things. Go figure. It used to be cool to say, "Yeah, I just got out of rehab." Now, for some, it's just a sign of poor choices and bad behavior.

After I graduated from college, and spent three months on my mother's couch, wondering where my life was going, and doing very little to get wherever that was exactly, I took her heartfelt advice: "Get a damn job!" And so I went in search of the one place I knew would be interesting and not pose a great deal of hard work, or so my one college professor, who taught Advertising 101, told us.

"If you want to look busy in an agency, or any company for that matter, simply carry a folder with you whenever you need to take a break, or just want to wander the halls. Furthermore," he continued, "this technique works extremely well if you want to gain entry to a large corporation where no one person knows everybody, so with file folder in hand, you could probably set up a desk, and get a phone, and a key to the executive washroom, just by looking like you belong." Naturally, we all thought he was kidding, but take my word for it, it happens.

Anyway, getting back to my current unemployed status, the only question the personnel lady asked me was "How fast do you type, Honey?" She was, and rightly so, unimpressed that I graduated in the bottom tenth of my class at the state university where I'd majored in Business Administration, having gone through every other major, including Art History and the prerequisite English Lit only to end up in an advertising class under the tutelage of a guy who was the prime example of those who teach because they cannot begin to do whatever it is they teach, and so forth. Fine. The reality was he was cute, and I was young, and it seemed like it would be fun.

I went on three interviews. The first one was for the Office Clerk to a woman who could best be described as grim. In fact, the name of the agency was "Noir" so that probably should have been my first clue as to the agency's culture. Let's just say it was not a match. She promised to get back to me, but I heard from my personnel rep that she thought I was too "peppy." Thank freakin' God...

The second interview was no better. The woman I would work for was the Executive Secretary to the head of the agency which bore his name, along with two other Gents. She was a very serious individual who obviously needed help, judging from the piles and piles of paperwork that seemed to be engulfing her desk and threatened to block any attempt at getting to the credenza, let alone file in it.

My meeting with her boss was spent mostly trying to make eye contact with him since he seemed fixated on the tight black turtleneck sweater I was wearing that day; asking me all about my social life, and if the presence of a boyfriend would interfere with the many long hours I would likely be spending on the latest campaign or new business pitch. "We tend to pull all-nighters here. But don't worry, that's part of the fun."

Yea, more fun!

Anyway, she said she would get back to me, and did about three weeks after I got my first job as the Floater at O'Reilly, Kensington & Partners, working for a lovely woman whose father was rumored to be in the Mafia, and who wanted everyone who worked for her to consider taking the "est" training, of which she was a huge devotee. I did attend about five "Guest Seminars" and actually met Werner Erhard in the flesh, but by that time, I "Got It" and was quite content with my job as the Fill-in-Babe for those who are out sick or on vacation, or just need a mental health day.

I learned a lot in the weeks and months ahead, about

every department and the type of personality that is drawn to work in each one. Account Services: logical, structured, follows instructions well, thinks they are the most important person on the team. Creative: freethinker, spontaneous, anti-authority, knows they are the most important person on the team. Media: good at data analysis, problem solver, hopes they are the most important person on the team. Traffic: fluid thinker, able to establish patters, doesn't care if they are the most important person on the team. Production: all-of-the-above, etc. But the most important lesson was about New Business and how this drives the heartbeat of any agency.

In fact, there are really only two main objectives in every agency:

Objective #1: Keep The Clients You Have

No matter what it takes, no matter to what extreme you must go to keep your current stable of clients so happy they don't, for even one moment, think to bring their Account into review and ruin your rating in one of the several ad agency tabloids. Nothing hurts worse than a mediocre "C+."

Objective #2: Get New Clients

One might ask how this system survives, if everyone is working their damnedest to meet both goals simultaneously. In the perfect advertising world (which does not exist, by the way, except in the minds of agency honchos and MBA candidates,) there would be enough clients to go around so that everyone would be content to turn out the most clever, most insightful, most effective and award winning ads which catapult their client's sales through the roof, and not be overly concerned about beating the bushes for fresh meat; everyone slaving to get that prize client which can be held up with pride to the ad community as a whole – a place where the "What have you done lately" mantra is something we all live by and in fear of.

Sadly, many ads and campaigns are dreck; half-witted attempts at humor, written and approved on the basis of ego rather than examples of a solid ad, a smart ad, a true statement and not BS, or one that is marked by embarrassing condescension – one that is both informative and persuasive, told from a "speak with one voice" community of talented creatives and account types who are sincere in the work they do and the words they write; supported by a crack team of well-trained and dedicated Media, Traffic, Production, Information Management, Finance, Personnel and Office Services groups.

Now, as you have probably guessed, I cannot write an ad, good or bad, so take what I say with a bit of tongue-in-cheek. Mine is merely a consumer's point of view, having been tested and tried in a most out-of-the-ordinary industry – if one is into insufficient pay, unending pressure and long hours without so much as a "thank you" for said efforts. So allow me to properly introduce myself; I am TOM ... a pleasure meeting you.

I got my job at HIP, Inc. thanks, in part, to the previous Office Manager's timely nervous breakdown. Apparently, the agency had just been through a particularly grueling office move, and one day she went out for a long lunch never to be seen or heard from again. For the first few days, everyone assumed she was just hiding out to avoid the fallout of decisions "The Powers That Be" (hereafter referred to as TPTB,) dictated but she would take the heat for. No one found out she had tossed all her office files, until I started, only to find no paperwork, no Rolodex, no calendar, no vendor contracts, no floor plans, nada. Thank goodness her nifty IBM Selectric II typewriter was still there because, thanks to my aforementioned typing skills, I set about writing and sending out a plethora of Inter-Office Memos undoing all the chaos and confusion she left behind, and became TOM, The Office Mom.

So, welcome to Adland! Please stay seated, keep your hands inside the vehicle, and crank up your favorite '80s hit, because in the immortal words of Marge Channing, played by that ultimate Babe, Ms. Bette Davis, *"Fasten your seat belts. It's going to be a bumpy night."*

Chapter 2

A POLAROID IS WORTH A THOUSAND WORDS

For your listening pleasure: *"Working for the Weekend" - Loverboy*

Quote for the day: *"It's so BIG!"*

*I*t's a typical Monday morning and the status meeting attendees straggle into Conference Room Alpha, each expounding the previous weekend's conquest of Ecstasy, both physical and pharmaceutical. Comparing notes about which club had the best DJ, the hottest-looking crowd and a free flow of all you can snort, imbibe, or smoke. Two complain how their paltry weekly paychecks translate to only one pair of decent designer shoes ... dare we say "knock-offs?"

Not that it matters, since these musings are confined to the Tots in Adland. The real heavy hitters, Babes, Players and Gents, remain silent behind their sunglasses, tight-lipped except for the faint whirring of a pager set on vibrate, the faint warble of some top-ten hit playing on a Walkman, or the occasional sip of java, courtesy of the new office *grind-your-own-beans-from-Hawaii* coffee maker, all the while waiting for the caffeine to mingle with a couple of vitamin B-12's and the *Jolt Cola* already coursing through their veins. It is here where the real power lies behind an Account traversing the maze from concept to execution.

"So, does everyone have a status sheet?" asks Vicki, Director of Traffic.

"Why do we have to get these pages anyway? It's all on our PCs. Can't we just refer to that when we get back to our desks? It's such a waste of trees!"

"Where the fuck are the plain bagels? Don't we have anything besides onion, poppy and sesame seeds? I have diverticulitis, for Christ's sake. And who eats blueberry bagels, anyway? Blueberries belong in a muffin...Hello?"

"It's cold in here. I'm freezing my ass off. Didn't anyone call Office Services yet?"

"I guess Nadine is not coming? I heard she and Josh got together this weekend ... and her car is still in the parking lot downstairs. Can we say ... hangover?"

"Can we say ... love? What's wrong with that? Don't any of you people believe in love?"

"Does anybody know a good herbalist? My guy got deported on Saturday, can you believe that shit?"

And so on for at least the first ten minutes while everyone decompressed and drank their coffee and settled into office mode.

Emily, or in tighter circles, "EM," slipped in the side door of the conference room, always late for the morning meetings, though in the early stages of a politically correct world no one wanted to "ask" or "tell" and really no one cared...your business is yours. She took her place just as the meeting took on a semblance of formality...such as it is in Adland.

She was the Brad Pitt of lesbians...before that awful

beard and 29 children...with an appealing and perfect face; paying tribute to Hesse's description of Siddartha's mother – *"somehow at once masculine and feminine, and yet neither one nor the other,"* and blessed with the most attractive features, those of symmetry and the wide eyes so engaging in the cutest puppy of the litter and babies who really do deserve the gush of "Oh, what a pretty face!" (Not at all like Winston Churchill or E.T., which is what most babies actually look like, only no one has the *chutzpah* to tell their ametropic parents.)

Her attraction to the female form had evolved (coupled with her DNA) out of a natural repulsion women, hetero and not, sometimes feel the first time they see the male S-E-X organ. Particularly if the first time they get this glimpse, it is peeing or engaged in a well-practiced, self-absorbed, one-handed activity men favor. She was secretly in lust with a Babe I have christened "Illegally Blonde," but then who on the staff wasn't?

Meanwhile, down the hall, in Creative, another conversation, so typical in Adland, was taking place...

"So, in essence, you are telling me that what I am experiencing as the shower scene in *Psycho* is not something I should be concerned about? Are you insane?"

Claire, who as of thirty minutes ago was the Group Head for the Design Group in charge of all the client brochures, had just been told she is being moved out of her group entirely without so much as a "Wham, Bam, Thank You, Ma'am."

Sadly, it was not Claire who was insane. She just worked in a looney bin, run by the inmates. Such is Adland, a place not unlike Wonderland, where the Mad Hatter has a tea party and calls it a day's work, and everyone had better be mindful of their heads (both kinds) lest they be lopped off at the most inopportune moment.

"Well, no, not exactly," said Randolph "Call me Randy" Railsback, VP of Client Services for an account I'll tell you about shortly. "It's just that we all decided this would be more efficient."

"More efficient? Was it "efficient" eighteen months ago when I was asked to take this sad, pathetic excuse of a department in hand and set down some guidelines and expectations for what has become, under **my** management, I remind you, the singularly most efficient group in the entire so-called Creative Department?"

"It's not that we don't appreciate your efforts, Claire." He said in his usual cheerful, but utterly dim-witted tone. "After all, we want you to stay and work that same magic with the corporate training manuals, as you did with the brochures. So you moving back to the Account side is really a promotion of sorts."

"A promotion comes with an increase in salary. Exactly how much of a promotion are we talking about?"

"Now, I really can't get into that," said Randy, in his best backpedal voice. "It all depends on how well you do in your new job."

"So any credit for what I have accomplished these many months is going to that back-biting little turd who is now the head of **my** group?!?!" By now Claire was spitting into the handset.

No wonder they always tell you these things over the phone, on their way to a meeting or lunch, rather than have the *cojones* to give you the news face-to-face. So much more efficient that way, and I suppose kinder than getting a voice mail message, especially since the hard-copy memo about the new Group Head is already in the inter-office mail.

As every Babe will tell you, "To succeed at HIP, Inc., it pays to have a dick or know how to blow one." And Claire, capable and committed to task though she was, unfortunately didn't and wouldn't. Ah — but what she did have was something even better. She had moxie, she had intelligence and drive ... and more important, she had a collection of some pretty steamy Polaroids taken at last year's after-club activities which followed what are always Adland's most notorious Christmas parties.

"'All's fair in love and war,' and I have the pictures to prove it!" she thought. And she was patient. She would have her moment, but for now she would need to start packing and move to the Account Services floor. She was a Creative no more.

Meanwhile, up two floors and behind a pair of frosted glass doors opening to a large oval-shaped room, of which one wall was floor-to-ceiling windows overlooking the spectacular cityscape, the senior partners and department VPs were having their weekly powwow, and dissecting their latest in a recent and worrisome streak of New Business losses...

"It's no secret we should have gotten that Account. We did our very best to please and give them exactly what they wanted," said Mr. Hamilton.

Never mind that what that particular client wanted was a lie not even we could tell with a straight face, nor would any self-respecting consumer buy the product without subsequently considering a class action suit. We got sued... a lot. Often enough for Reception to have our legal firm, Biddleman, Shaft, Dodger & Partners, on 1-Touch Dialing. But then that goes along with having one of the biggest quasi-pharmaceutical companies in the world as your number-one client.

In fact, without said client, HIP, Inc., would cease to exist. Oh, sure, we had other clients and some were actually profitable, but the truth was, without Prichard-Bailey Industries, makers of everything from **GETNOGAS**, a remarkable little pill that keeps bouts of flatus at bay, to **THICK 'N LUSH,** a hair restoration gel, and their biggest seller of all time, **RAMROD**, the herbal equivalent of what would become known as Viagra, we would go belly up in as little time as it took to hand out the last paycheck and sell all the assets for pennies-on-the-dollar at one of those cringe-worthy going-out-of-business auctions.

Perhaps you'd like to see the script from the Ramrod commercial that won us this account? (Please forgive the makeshift format.)

:30 Commercial/TV#PBI-RR-1975-00719

ACCOUNT:	PBI
PRODUCT:	RAMROD
CW:	Jackson, Chris
AD:	Hilliard, Brice
ACCT. EX:	Railsback, "Randy"

VISUAL:

Split screen showing two young, sexy women talking to each other on the phone; each one holding a wedding photo featuring them and their not-so-young husbands.

A petite blonde wearing a short silk robe, over tight jeans, bare feet, hair wrapped in a towel; sweet, high-pitched voice

AUDIO:

"It's so BIG!"

VISUAL:

"Feline" brunette, business suit and very high heels, which she kicks off as she curls up on a leather sofa.

AUDIO:

"I can't believe how long it lasted."

VISUAL:

Blonde, unwrapping her hair and shaking her head.

AUDIO:

"If I'd known it would be this good, I'd have done it sooner."

VISUAL:

Brunette taking a long all-body stretch.

AUDIO:

"Me, too. I can't wait to try it again."

VISUAL:

Camera pulls back to reveal they are talking about the newest, largest, scariest roller-coaster at the local family theme park, evidenced by the tee-shirt revealed when the blonde takes off her robe, and the theme-park cap the brunette puts on, each one emblazoned with "I Rode Gargantuan!"

They put their framed picture down and we see family shots of wife, husband and children for each of them.

VISUAL:

CUT TO product shot of RAMROD

ANNOUNCER V.O.:

"When you want to **be** Gargantuan, use RAMROD."

BLONDE V.O.:

"It's so BIG!"

FADE TO BLACK

Yeah, they all say that. But of course the real fear was that the senior partners at PBI were getting as old as the senior partners at HIP, Inc., and when one side or the other retired, some young-buck, hungry and truly talented agency would come along and simply present a better creative product for a cheaper rate.

So it goes in Adland, where only the strong and resourceful, or the weak and cunning survive.

But that's a story for another day ...

Chapter 3

BEST IN SHOW

For your listening pleasure: *"Another One Bites the Dust" - Queen*

Quote for the day: *"That thing creeps me out. I don't know whether to walk it or throw it a bone."*

They say men who have huge, impressive or aggressive dogs are really suffering from envy. The dog, its personality and all its relative proportions, including their "pole and tackle" set, if you will, represent everything the owner is not. Our client, Paxton, had such a dog; "Attila," the Saint Bernard.

Now why anyone would name a dog, renowned for its life-saving skills, after a fierce and bloodthirsty warrior is anyone's guess, but here's a clue...

"Paxton, **not** Mr. Paxton; that was my father," he'd say, making a sign of the cross. "And may he burn in H-E-double-L, for all of eternity."

Poor "Attila." He had been a roly-poly, furry and friendly gift from the dearly departed dad (now on perpetual holiday, it would appear, on the River Styx,) and was, in a not-so-subtle way, symbolic of how much said *paterfamilias* felt he was always coming to the rescue of his seemingly no-talent-for-business, ne'er-do-well son, who, upon said father's demise, sold all the family's stocks and bonds, sinking every dime into what became, in the mid-eighties, the most chic shoppe on Rodeo Drive.

Theodora's was the fashion home of the stars, the envy of every design house from Paris to New York, a destination highlighted on all the maps of 90210, and as far as Paxton was concerned, a huge middle finger to the memory of his father, whose once-revered, life-size portrait, which used to hang in the hallowed halls of the Jonathan Club, now hung in the communal dressing room, frequently used as a clothing rack, festooned with gowns, scarves, belts and lingerie.

Not that he was abusive to the dog in any way; quite the contrary. The dog was a prince among dogs; loved, pampered and catered to like no other dog that ever lived. He was served out of sterling silver bowls, feasting on hand-carved, slow-roasted meats, drinking water that came from glaciers in Iceland. He rode in style in one of Paxton's collection of Bentleys; to the vet, to the groomers, to the dog psychic, and the trainer; and right on into the conference rooms of HIP, Inc.

Too bad potty training was not big on the list of disciplines this creature was schooled in. "Oh, poor baby had to tinkle," soothed Paxton. Naturally, because I wanted to keep my job, I would echo the cooing sound and send for housekeeping as I put down copious layers of paper towels, all the while cursing the beast and the owner.

"Tinkle? It's more like a fucking monsoon," I said. "That damned dog has killed the last fichus. I swear, I'm getting a gun."

"Oh, you don't really mean that. You love dogs," said Frances, or as I called her, The Sphinx, our receptionist *extraordinaire.*

"Yes, I have three rescues, but they are all housebroken. They don't pee on my hardwood or my oriental rugs, or in my planters; they don't take a dump on the limestone flooring, or in Mr. Hamilton's office...oh, okay, well maybe that one time when we had a 'Bring Your Pet to Work Day,' but he never seems to mind when it's Attila."

"Well, naturally, it's a $69 million account. As far as he's concerned, the dog could bite him and draw blood, and unless he came down with rabies, that would be just fine, because ..."

"Here at HIP, Inc., **anything** that makes our clients happy, makes us happy!" We say in unison.

"God, I need a vodka."

And then one day my prayers, and all the prayers of anyone who had the misfortune of getting peed on, or farted at, or drooled over, or whose new and expensive designer suit was covered in long brown, tan and white hair after a conference meeting with this client and his canine cohort, came true – Attila had a stroke and died.

Unfortunately, it was in the middle of our presentation to Paxton for the coming year's campaign.

We sent an ostentatious spray of white roses to the memorial service, and a condolence card crafted by the Print Production Department, dutifully signed by everyone even remotely related to work on the Paxton account. The client was in mourning and quite indisposed at his villa in the south of France, while his many assistants (fashion whores, the lot of them,) managed the account as well as the many displays and offerings of sympathy that poured in from around the world for the next several weeks. The tabloid and fashion rags ate it up. Meanwhile, we were dancing in our workstations, quietly humming "Ding, dong, the dog is dead!"

Imagine, then, my surprise, when, some months later, on a Tuesday, in Conference Room Delta, where we were prepping for the usual Paxton client meeting ...

"Greetings, all!" That raspy little voice called out. "I have a surprise for you."

Being one who loathes surprises of any kind, I (being borderline obsessive-compulsive, and this long before it became a well-known disease, so that everyone who knew me just thought I was an A-#1 bitch,) peeked out into the reception area and to my horror saw Attila sitting at his master's heel.

"What the fuck?" I said, probably louder than I meant to, and ducked back around the corner.

"Yes, he **is** so lifelike, isn't he? It's almost like having him back with me." Paxton began to snivel and pulled out an Hermès scarf, blowing his nose and rooting out both nostrils. "That is exactly what they guaranteed me he would be like." He said. Speaking to Frances, whose expression that day, as always, rivaled The Sphinx in its timeless, non-judgmental serenity.

"Well, Paxton, so good to have you back! I got your message and wanted to come out and personally thank you for this thoughtful gift," said Mr. Hamilton, at his vocal best, sounding just like a game-show host. "We will search out a special place for Attila here," he said, patting the dog on top of its head. "Yes, we certainly will find a place for him." (In one of our basement storage lockers, no doubt, dragging it out and dusting it off just before the biweekly account meeting ... please, please, please.)

"Well, actually ..." Paxton began as he spun around to survey the reception area seating.

"Don't say it. If there is a god, may she strike you dead before you say what I think you are going to say," I thought.

"Right here is where I had in mind. Right here next to the Queen Anne chair, as though he was at the right hand of his master, waiting to fetch his pair of slippers." He was practically choking back the tears at this point.

"Sonofabitch!" That scuzzy thing next to my newly delivered, custom made, slightly oversize Queen Anne chair upholstered in hand brushed, double napped, 100% fine suit-quality, gray flannel???? My head was exploding not to shout this out, as I walked up, feigning a self-medicated smile, having just popped whatever pill, fuzzy though it might be, was in my left jacket pocket.

"Excellent. We'll just get a pair and place them right next to good 'ol Attila, then, won't we, TOM?"

"Of course we will. I'll be happy to take care of that." (It's not pretty being easy, but somebody's got to do it.)

"I'll send over a pair from the store this afternoon, something Italian." Paxton said now, more composed, with a quick toss of the hand to no one in particular. And as they walked to the conference room, Mr. Hamilton's arm around Paxton's shoulder, Paxton leaned in ever so slightly, soaking in the comforting, almost fatherly gesture.

"That thing creeps me out. I don't know whether to walk it or throw it a bone."

"At least it won't pee on the carpet anymore," said The

Sphinx, smiling her best Mona Lisa smile. Only God or the Devil ever knew what she was really thinking. It was her charm and her strength. She was a Babe among Babes.

But that's a story for another day ...

Chapter 4

FAIREST LADY

For your listening pleasure: *"I've Been Waiting for a Girl Like You - Foreigner*

Quote for the day: *"I swear, Elliott, I didn't know she was a man, or I wouldn't have hooked you up!"*

Poor Professor Higgins, whilst in pursuit of transforming Eliza Doolittle from a guttersnipe to a duchess, asks, "Why can't a woman be more like a man?" Could it be because in the hearts and souls of most females, this would be construed as a step back in the evolutionary chain?

Men are driven by their primal urges and are intent to have S-E-X and make war with equal fervor. Women, on the other hand, are usually motivated by a more subtle set of priorities; self-actualization, home, family, security, friendship; continually honing the fine art of negotiation so that matter and anti-matter do not meet in their universe. But we, as a society have convinced ourselves, unwisely, that everyone should be the same, and there is no difference between men and women, any more than there is a difference between someone who is white and someone who is black, brown, yellow, red, or any combination thereof.

I have always lived my life knowing that race is not and never shall be a point of inequality, and one thing I am equally certain of is there is a true and abiding difference between the sexes. The Feminist Movement missed the mark on that one tiny point, I'm afraid. Equal pay for equal work, count me in! Women are no different from men ... bullshit.

And the saying about never judging a book by its cover must always and especially apply to the individual since you never really know what lies behind the face or fashion of anyone you meet; even a person you see and work with on a daily basis. The truth is you never know what secrets people have and God knows everyone is entitled to them.

"Someone is leaving pee on the toilet seat again. Please find out who it is and make them stop!"

This is one of the hundreds of requests my team and I handle every week; some sublime, most ridiculous.

"What the hell am I supposed to do, camp out in the Ladies' Room and peek discretely under the stall doors every time someone takes a piss?" I asked Frances during one of our fireside chats, as I sat in the guest chair next to her.

The stylish and imposing reception station was manned at various times with up to three attendants; Frances, a Floater, who, if they are doing their job at all, was almost never seated there, but instead was working one of the many support positions throughout the agency, and one of two part-time receptionists who were job-sharing. Usually these were students or interns, or a combination of both. That accounts for three chairs, but the fourth chair is the guest chair and it is periodically filled by anyone and everyone in the agency who need a moment of repose or counsel from Frances, our in-house Oracle, or as I like to call her, The Sphinx.

Frances came to HIP, Inc. in the dawn of the '80s, an ex-, ex-, ex-wife of a not-to-be-named '60s rock star whose band once filled the Forum, the Long Beach Arena and the Hollywood Bowl all in the same week. Alas, fame, like fortune, doesn't last forever and the day came when Frances received the terrible news of her ex, thrice-removed, the way most everyone did...on MTV. Apparently he, and what was left of his band, had been relegated to playing small, more "intimate" venues...aka...Keno lounges at the retirement communities in Palm Springs, and whilst smashing up his guitar at the end of his signature song, keeled over on stage in front of a crowd of similarly aged fans who thought it was all a new ending to an old and well-rehearsed act. It took them several minutes to realize the curtain had literally come down, this time permanently.

All three of the wives, each from a successively younger generation, attended the funeral and paid homage to their former spouse, with phrases like "awesome," "stud," "genius," "mentor," "cosmic," "tantric," etc., etc. If only Frances had been less in love/lust when she was a young bride, because though she had put up with the most crap in their early years and wrote most of the lyrics of his hit songs, she received very little in the end: a few trinkets, some photos, and enough to pay off her digs in Laurel Canyon. Her lawyer said he would begin work on royalty rights, but not to count on anything, and maybe she should find work until he had some good news.

Meanwhile, HIP, Inc. needed a Receptionist and Frances had a look that went with the furniture ... serene, classy and with just enough sex appeal to be charming, engaging and welcoming. That she had a formidable IQ, was extremely well-educated, possessed a photographic memory, and had actually been a *Jeopardy!* contestant was a secret she shared with only a select few. She was the only person I ever knew who was, at once, perspicacious, and could use the word correctly in a sentence. Her job was to speak and appear as the delightful "voice and face" of HIP, Inc. to the clients, media reps, and every other manner of visitor to the agency. She did her job well, and got paid a pittance, but then this is Adland, and only those involved in the process of producing an ad have a hope in hell of ever making any real money. The rest of us are clearly in it for the "fun."

"Besides which, it's happening in more than one bathroom on more than one floor. Whoever this person is, they travel around a lot. I'm getting notes from Account Services all the way to Finance."

"Yes, but right now we have more guys in that group and the women have been there long enough for me to know it can't be one of them."

"Perhaps one of the guys is playing a sick joke by sneaking into the Ladies' Room?"

"No, they tried that last year and I told those involved I would personally nail the culprit to the bathroom vestibule wall, naked from the waist down, with a sign posted above their heads that was to be read aloud by every female who walked in; 'Well, it looks like a penis,' as they hold up their pinkie finger."

"I see. By the way, you'll never guess who came in as VP on Ramrod."

"Who?"

"Elliott Monroe."

"Are you fucking kidding me? Didn't he just get canned on the Centurion account for that last scandal? I mean really, it's a regional business, who was going to believe he needed to go on a location scouting trip to Bangkok? I heard *Harmony Springs* in Malibu named a group session room after him he was there so often. What's he doing here on the agency side?"

"Apparently, this last intervention convinced TPTB he'd be perfect for this job, so we wooed him to help Randy on Ramrod. Randy, poor lamb, is not the 'young stud' he used to be and Elliott better fit the profile for who should work on it."

"A lean, mean fucking machine?"

We laugh.

But truly, that is what you have to project to the client on this particular account, otherwise, what's the point? If you don't look like you have a constant hard-on, or at least act like you can hoist up ye ol' mainsail at a moment's notice, you will not be taken seriously on Ramrod.

Tales of sexual conquest notwithstanding, everyone who works on this peachy account, whether male or female (for obvious reasons, mostly male,) must look like they can "get some" on a regular basis, and Monday morning Staff Meetings are rife with stories about who got what from whom. No salacious detail is too raw, too overt, or even too unbelievable (threesomes ... sheep ... E.T.s ... anyone?) to be withheld. The more offensive, the better one's standing in the group.. And if you are lucky or just plain tacky, word of your exploits will get back to the client and you will have scored even more points, for yourself and the agency.

Elliott Monroe used to work the client side of the business for another of HIP, Inc.'s roster of clients, but one stint too many in rehab for addictions ranging from alcohol to drugs, to gambling to drugs, to anger issues to drugs, and finally S-E-X addition and of course, drugs, landed him, through a series of networking and probably blackmail, as the newest Sr. Account Manager on Ramrod. A match made in heaven.

"Men are scum."

Actually, in all fairness, that is not entirely true. It just seems that way if you are one of the very few women assigned to work as an assistant or a coordinator on this account. You enter a time warp, and arrive somewhere between The Stone Age, and the formation of N.O.W. in the mid-'60s, having entirely skipped over women getting the vote in 1920, or the creation of the Pill or pantyhose, two things no self-respecting Babe would be without.
things no self-respecting Babe would be withoutthings no self-respecting Babe would be without

~~~

Lorelei waited until everyone had left for lunch before she went to the Ladies' Room. She smiled each time she saw the universal sign for female on the door. It gave her hope. Soon it would be true in every sense of the word, but for now, she still felt a bit like a fraud. She was on the final lap of her journey to becoming what she always knew she was ... a woman.

She was nine when she realized the image in the mirror

staring back at her was inaccurate. She was not the "little man" her mother doted on, nor was she the son of a proud father, engaging the child in every sport known to mankind; from baseball, to football, hunting and the like. Not that she lacked athletic skills, but she would have rather been a ballet dancer than a first baseman. She had lived a life of confusion for herself and those around her, who sensed something was not as it should be, and coming from a small Midwestern town in the very buckle of the "Bible Belt" made it all the worse. When she turned 18, she left, never to return, changed her name and began to save up to correct her sex. Lorelei was transgender.

She was also a top-notch Account Coordinator and knew as much about the Ramrod business as any man who worked on the account. An Uber-Babe, she was a petite, caramel-hued knockout with raven hair and a killer figure. That she was soft-spoken and reserved in both dress and manner belied a high IQ and a keen, competitive nature, intent on flying below the radar until her ultimate mission could be accomplished. Her year of living as a woman was almost up and then she would face her final evaluation for sexual reassignment surgery. She would have no trouble passing the test.

That is, until the client decided it would be nice to have an out-of-town weekend conference, so that everyone on the team could "bond." A flaccid excuse, if you ask me, to get the men and the women on the account in the same hotel at the same time.

"Excuse me, but may I ask a question?" Lorelei said as she sat in the guest chair.

"Of course you may. How may I help?"

"I was wondering if you thought there was any legitimate reason for me to bow out of this Ramrod Team weekend? I don't exactly feel comfortable with the idea of it."

"Nor should you, my dear. It's simply fraught with peril, if truth be told. But I guess the beach party they threw last year didn't go far enough in the 'bonding' department. So, unless you want to be thought of as a poor sport and lose your job, or you come down with chicken pox by Friday, I suggest you go – sip water on ice instead of vodka on the rocks, keep your door locked and your wits about you."

"I see your point. I guess that means I'll be going. I don't want to get fired."

Frances felt especially fond of this young woman, as it was she who would first meet her that morning nearly a year ago when she, arriving early as usual, found Lorelei standing at the front doors waiting for the agency to open. She had an interview with Human Resources (or Human Remains, depending on your dealings with them,) and did not want to be late. It was 8:45 a.m. when The Sphinx arrived and Lorelei's appointment was not until 9:30 a.m., so there was plenty of time to talk and see if she was more than just a stunning face. She was sweet, funny and bright, and obviously well read and educated, picking up on every literary, political and film reference that Frances was known to pepper her speech with. Frances liked her immediately and was pleased to see her hired, even if it was for the dreadful Ramrod account.

"You'll be fine. You go and have a good time and stay safe. If absolutely necessary, dial 911," Frances said. "And it couldn't hurt to carry mace."

The shocked expression on Lorelei's face made Frances want to laugh and cry, out of compassion, but instead she told her she was only kidding about the mace. (As for me, I would have advised bringing a baseball bat and aiming low, but then no one ever asked me to "bond" with them in all the years I worked in Adland, except one time and that is definitely a story for another day.)

Friday afternoon came late for some and far too early for others in the Ramrod Account Group..

Randy had his bag packed since the trip was announced in Monday's client Status Meeting, and that all would be riding aboard a luxury party bus to the local mountain resort for a weekend of fun and games, and a chance for the Account Team to "bond."

Elliott brought his usual luggage, a *Gucci* briefcase, which contained a flask, a box of condoms and one change of underwear. Anything else he figured he could buy at the Winslow Lodge Hunting and Fishing Shoppe. He intended to do some hunting this weekend and had already set his sights on a lovely doe – Lorelei.

Lorelei brought a sensible overnight bag packed with sensible things, including two changes of daytime clothing, consisting of tee-shirts, shorts and jeans, a go-anywhere basic black sheath dress which could be dressed up or down, a pair of pajamas, and a can of mace.

"So, who do you think you'll end up with?" one of the Babes asked aloud, as they put the final touches on their makeup in the bathroom, moments before the "all aboard" was announced.

"Does it matter?" Illegally Blonde asked. "As long as everyone has a good time."

"Did anyone remember to bring salt for the margaritas this time? I've got the ice and the mix in my cooler."

"I brought the Jell-O shots, guac and the chips."

"Blue Agave or Cuervo?"

"Both, naturally."

"This is going to be an awesome ride!"

"I'm doomed," Lorelei thought. But she put on a smile and somehow managed to enjoy the bus ride up the mountain without incident.

Elliott could not take his eyes off her. She was not like the other gals on the account. She was classy and smart. "Too smart for a girl," Elliott thought. "She needs a man to bring out her real talents."

(I have to just say this ... if this Gent, and I use the word with the utmost sense of irony ... had an idea in his head that didn't involve S-E-X, it would perish from lack of any other brain cell to copulate with and reproduce. But then, as I explained earlier, this is why he was chosen to work on this account.)

"Cutting one out of the herd, eh?" Randy said. "I've got my eye on Illegally Blonde over there. Of course she's fair game now that Mr. Hamilton's has moved on, so I figure what the hell? Why not give it a shot?"

"Go for it, man." Elliott said encouragingly, but in his head he was getting a kick out of seeing this aging stallion even think he could score with such a firecracker, even if she was a "free agent," so to speak. Her now fizzled affair with Mr. Hamilton's was widely known throughout HIP, Inc., and Adland in general due to the incestuous nature of our business. It didn't hurt that our offices were down the street from a small, boutique hotel which catered to the very discreet and where we had a suite for "out of town" guests, though mostly in-town guests used it. It was an entertainment write-off and entertainment is exactly what TPTB engaged in when frequenting the place for some afternoon delight.

I won't bore you with all the mundane details of what happened when they arrived except to say the first night was pretty civilized with a sit-down dinner and then an early turn-in. The next day, Saturday, would consist of team activities set up by the resort and an outside consultant hired to coach the Account Team in various games, assignments and competitions directed towards building a framework of camaraderie and trust. That night there would be the blowout party with a cocktail hour, buffet dinner and dancing.

Lorelei was already dressed and ready to go downstairs when she heard a knock at her door. "Who's there?" No reply. "Who's out there?" Lorelei asked again, as she looked through the dirty peephole. "What do you want?"

"For God's sake, open the door, Lorelei, I'm freezing my ass off out here!"

It was Illegally Blonde. Lorelei opened the door to find her co-worker wrapped in a towel, carrying a plastic Ziploc bag full of toiletries, a white cotton dress and a pair of black patent-leather stilettos.

"Thank you. I was beginning to think I would die of old age out there. Got anything to drink?"

"Uh, no, not really, other than what might be in the refrigerator. But I don't have a key."

"Oh, that's okay, sweetie, I learned to pick a lock when I was five. My Daddy was the town's locksmith." And so taking a hairpin out of her little bag, she deftly opened the lock and took out four vodka bottles, drinking two in rapid succession.

"Do you want one?"

"No, thank you." Lorelei said, afraid to ask why her guest was only wearing a towel. "I don't really drink."

"Yeah, I noticed that on the way up here. You aren't much of a party animal, are you?" Illegally Blonde laughed a little and then downed the other two little bottles.

"I guess not."

"That's too bad, because you are a really cute girl, and it wouldn't hurt your job ops any, if you get what I'm saying."

"I think I know what you mean. By the way, would you like my robe?"

"Oh, yeah, sorry. I need to use your shower, if you don't mind. My lame excuse for a roommate is still in there and at the rate she is going, I won't make the cocktail hour. Do you mind? I heard you got a room to yourself, and you look like you're all set to go, and I figured you're the type to leave a bathroom clean after you use it."

"Flattery will get you everywhere," thought Lorelei. "Sure, go right ahead."

"Come in with me?" Illegally Blonde beckoned as she threw back the shower curtain and dropped her towel on the floor.

"I beg your pardon?"

"Come in and sit on the loo and talk to me, silly. I won't bite."

Lorelei went in, and placing a dry towel on the seat of the commode, sat down, trying not to look in the direction of the shower; but since the opposite wall was floor-to-ceiling mirror, no matter where she looked, she could see the outline of Illegally Blonde's body. Voluptuous did not begin to describe her.

"I'm glad all that game crap is done with, aren't you?"

"Didn't you care for it?"

"HELL no! I particularly object to hanging from a rope and sliding across a ravine. What if I'd fallen? What if the rope broke? What if those '*dummkopfs*' at the other end failed to catch me? Then what?"

"Well, we were strapped in pretty well, and there was a safety line..."

"Fuck that. The only person I can count on to protect me is me."

She had a point there. Illegally Blonde exited the shower, dried off and asked Lorelei for the towel she was sitting on so she could wrap up her hair. Lorelei sat on the bed closest to the bathroom door.

"You've got to take control of the situation, you know? Have all the angles figured out in your mind ahead of time so that when things happen you've already been down that road or this road and you know what to do. Doesn't that make better sense?"

"I think that is exactly what today's exercises were designed to teach us: self-reliance and team trust."

"Trust!? Don't ever trust anyone who works here. That's the last thing you should do, especially the men. We all know where they are coming from and where they want to get to. Hand me my dress, would you?"

Lorelei did and then the shoes; she noticed there was no underwear in the bag.

"Don't wear 'em." Illegally Blonde said as if anticipating the question.

"Oh."

"Listen, you're welcome to any "goodies" in that brown bottle – Xanax, Ludes, Valium. I've got coke for later. Help yourself. Only stay away from the blue pills, those are my sleeping pills and they pack a wallop."

A few minutes passed as the hair dryer did its job and out from the steam came Illegally Blonde in a snug, white, spaghetti strapped dress that did little to conceal the fact that she was not wearing a bra, let alone panties. It was more than obvious she was a natural blonde.

"Shall we go?"

Lorelei was amazed at how little make-up her guest wore, that she hadn't spent more than a couple of minutes on her hair and that she was practically naked; moreover, she was beautiful, naturally beautiful even if she was a little older than you might guess.

"What?" Illegally Blonde asked, noticing that Lorelei was giving her the once-over.

"Nothing, I'm sorry. It's just that you look so..."

"Hot?" Illegally Blonde laughed. "You're not gay, are you? Because I don't go for that type, but I could introduce you to someone I know who might be perfect for you. And she works in Adland."

"No, I'm not gay."

"Well, I'm sure Elliott would be relieved to hear that. The buzz is he is on the prowl for you, girl, so you better be prepared."

"Thanks, I will," said Lorelei, swallowing hard. "Any words of advice?"

"Yeah. If you can't 'blind them with your brilliance, baffle them with your bullshit.'"

The music was throbbing; the food tantalizing, and the drinks were flowing so fast the bartender was coming down with carpal tunnel. Everyone had their game face on and pairs began to form.

Lorelei was hoping to be the wallflower in the group, but just as she thought to take flight back up to her room, Elliott walked up and asked her to dance.

"So, Randy tells me you are the best Account Coordinator he's ever known. That's high praise. Do you think you deserve it?"

Lorelei didn't know quite how to take this backhanded compliment. "I do my best," came to mind, and then, remembering Illegally Blonde's words of wisdom, "Yes, I think so."

Elliott was impressed. And she was giving him a hard-on.

"How about we take this party up to my room?" Elliott asked as he whisked her off the dance floor. Lorelei found herself led like a lamb to the slaughter. Time to take control. "How about my room, instead?"

"Well, all right! Lead on ..."

So they went to her room and one thing was beginning to lead to another until she slipped him a cocktail fit for a sleazeball, concocted from a sampling of Illegally Blonde's pill stash. He didn't taste a thing, having killed all his taste buds earlier in the evening with a bottle of Scotch and a cigar. And as he melted into the floor, he didn't feel anything either.

And then Lorelei did what Babes have been doing from

Eve to Cleopatra, from Marilyn to Madonna – she faked it.

It was the Royal Flush of Fakes, complete with moans, and groans, and a banging headboard as Elliott lay passed out on the floor, the tiniest of drool draining from the corner of his mouth, the bottle of *Absolut* he'd brought with him now empty in his hand. (Lorelei had poured the contents into the sink, swishing the last bit in her mouth before spitting it out.)

She tossed the bedding around the room and overturned one of the chairs; her shoes and clothing made a path around the room. She ran the shower once again, dampening the rest of the towels, save one, which she threw over Elliott's backside, having removed his clothing, throwing them hither-and-yon as well.

Applying a copious layer of lipstick, she went about pressing her lips on the sheets and pillowcases, on the glassware and all over Elliott's face and various other private parts.

He snored through the whole time. "Not very flattering," Lorelei laughed to herself.

She found a particularly graphic film on the Adult Cable channel and paid for four viewings, charging the expense to Elliott's corporate AMEX.

After that she took advantage of the chaise lounge by the window and had a smoke. "I'm spent!" She laughed again, looking over at Elliott, who was sleeping like a baby. "Was it good for you, too?"

Tightening the belt of her robe, grabbing a red Pashmina from the floor, and wrapping it across her lap, she felt comfortable enough to sleep, certain the effects of the drugs would not wear off until morning. She was a light sleeper anyway and would be awake and down to breakfast long before Elliott began to stir.

~~~

Fast-forward six months ...

No one knows where the rumor began, only that it finally made its way to the Monday morning client Status Meeting for Ramrod. From within the walls of Conference Room Omega, came a loud, blood-curdling yelp, followed by a deafening silence. And then Randy's voice. "I swear, Elliott, I didn't know she was a man, or I wouldn't have hooked you up!"

The Sphinx and I decided it didn't matter who started it, only that it seemed very much like instant *Karma*, and we chose never to speak of it again.

Illegally Blonde became the new, one and only female Account Manager on Ramrod. Randy's status as Alpha M-A-L-E on the Account was restored and Elliott resigned due to "personal issues." Last we heard, after another trip to rehab in Malibu, he went on a hiking adventure to *Kathmandu* in search of "inner peace."

And Lorelei? We don't really know. She had disappeared from HIP, Inc., and the Adland community at large exactly one year to her date of hire. We hoped she was happy. She was a Babe we would never forget.

~~~

A huge bouquet of pale pink roses arrived for Illegally Blonde about a week after she had settled into her small, windowless office, complete with the one thing every Account Coordinator works their fingers to the bone to get – a door.

The consensus was, of course, that it was just another

token of lust from someone in the agency...probably Randy. Or maybe it was a gesture of "Job well done, ol' girl," from her previous paramour/mentor, Mr. Hamilton.

She opened the card, and in the loveliest of script, a simple note:

> *"Thank you for everything, and Good Luck! All the Brightest and the Best,*
> *L."*

But that's a story for another day ...

Chapter 5

PAINFUL ALLIANCES

For your listening pleasure: *"Whip It" - DEVO*

Quote for the day: *"First rule of being a good Dominatrix is not to divulge any of the names of your clients."*

Mr. Ingersoll liked his bourbon aged and his women young. As Sr. VP, Creative Director here at HIP, Inc., his was the final word on any creative concept that was ultimately sent to the client to review and hopefully approve. He'd been in Adland for many years, more years than he'd like to claim because looking young and vigorous was top on his list of priorities.

To that end he indulged in all types of beauty-enhancing treatments usually reserved for the fairer sex; Dead Sea Mud facials, seaweed wraps, weekly salt rubs and palm oil massages at the local spa, and for the relief of stress, which he knew was the biggest contributor to the lines on one's face, sessions with a Dominatrix.

Little did he know, and I wished I'd never found this out, the "Lady" of all things humiliating, kinky and downright nasty, just happened to be my next-door neighbor in the little complex I lived at, one block from the ocean in Venice Beach.

Friedrich, or "Freddie" as he was known, was the Adland equivalent of a savant; like Michael Jackson was to music, or Tiger Woods to golf, he was a genius when it came to award-winning and sales-producing ads for any client lucky enough to have him work on their business. His was a legendary rise, years ago, at CCR&D (Castle, Carruthers, Richmond and Dunn), from the lowliest of mailroom clerks to Creative Director in the corner office overlooking Madison Avenue in only 3 short years. He was the "bad boy" of Creative, using his odd looks and utterly boyish charms to get into the heart and soul of any client and spin that intimate knowledge into an ad that made women want the product, and men want the women who wanted the product.

I say odd because he suffered from a rather rare skin condition, *Alopecia*, in which a person loses most or all of their hair; in his case, all the hair on his perfectly sculpted head, and all of his body. He did have eyebrows, which would rival Andy Rooney's or Brezhnev's. Women loved to play with them. They also loved to play with his hairless penis, which was enormous, and although it did not rival the porn star John Holmes, it was, or so "they" say, very much in contention for the grand prize of cocks that could boink a man's own belly button. He had rapier wit and could use his pale blue eyes to charm the chrome off a bumper if need be.

Freddie Girls, as they were known, were the collection of young women over the years who had worked for him, first as his Personal Assistant, and then on to whatever creative position they were really after – Producer, Writer,

Art Director, Commercial Actress, whatever. Not that he chose them, they mostly chose him. It was a carefully and politically staged event among the Babes as to who would be the next one to sit outside his office. Although sometimes an outside hire was chosen as was the case with the latest Babe, Serena, who, although she was born and blue-blood bred from Darien, Connecticut, could, with her fabulously, natural pouty lips, charm the chrome off a bumper as well. She may have been born a WASP, but she was a street-walking pro behind closed doors, judging from the number of times she was in his office behind closed doors and how often they went to "lunch" together.

But really, no one cared. It was so routine at HIP, Inc. as with all other Adland sites in town and across the nation, that no one gave it a second thought, mainly because so many of TPTB had on-staff hookups of their own.

Looking after Mr. Ingersoll was, however, never boring...

"I have no idea how your car ended up in impound, but the tow yard said it was picked up in the projects in East LA."

"It was stolen."

"Oh, yeah, stolen, I see. Well, I'll be happy to go down and get it. I'll need an advance of $475. May I get you to sign the voucher? Also, I need your driver's license and a copy of the registration, which I'm sure I can get from Finance. Don't worry; I'll be sure to have it detailed out as well."

"That would be nice."

"Anything else, Mr. Ingersoll?"

"No, thank you, Tom."

Then there was the time he "lost" his luggage on the way

to an out-of-town Presentation ...

"They located your luggage at *Caesar's* in Vegas. I'll have it on the next plane to Toledo, in plenty of time for the client meeting, Mr. Ingersoll."

"Very nice, TOM, thank you."

Or the time he got arrested by the local police for crossing a police barricade during an armed robbery at the bank next door to us...

"Please have my briefcase messengered to the house. I'll work from home this afternoon."

"Are they releasing you on your own recognizance, Mr. Ingersoll?"

"No. Not really."

"Okay, I'll be down shortly with the bail and arrange for a car and driver to take you home."

"Thank you, TOM. That's so nice."

And then there were the calls about his wife ...

"Your wife called, Mr. Ingersoll. Her *Neiman's* card was denied...again. Pissed? Yes, I'd say she was pissed. Oh, no problem, sir, I gave the store your credit card number. What's that? Yes, of course ... have them raise the limit to $69K ... got it!"

"Good. Thank you, TOM."

Anyway, you get the picture.

As for Brigette, my neighbor, or as I'm sure her clients called her, Lady Brigette, I'm not sure how he found her; 976-SPANK, no doubt, but she was one busy woman and clients flowed through her tiny apartment like water over Niagara.

When she first moved in it was as the girlfriend of the son of the building's owner. Actually, he had two girlfriends living with him. Cassie, the CPA, and Brigette, the Dominatrix, who also happened to have a Ph. D. in cellular biology, though she told me once there was "no real money in it," other than research grants, so she took up what had been a family business back in Hamburg, spanking rich and powerful men. She made it clear, in her cute little German accent, that there was no S-E-X involved, that is to say, she did not have sex with any of her customers, in case I was worried about the police or anything. (What? Worried? Nah.)

She kept normal daytime business hours, never starting before 9:00 a.m., and ending around 4:00 p.m., well before her two roommates came home. She was also quite a gourmet chef, and when her last client hobbled out of her door and down our common walkway, quietly closing the gate behind him, she would begin to prepare the most delicious-smelling concoctions. Any leftovers she gave me, as much as it pained me to do so, were immediately tossed in the garbage disposal. *EEEEEEW!*

Anyway, she did very well for herself, judging by her clientele, some of whom I recognized as they came and went, on the days I stayed home sick, or was out simply for a "mental health" holiday. One was a rather young, very handsome gent who was on one of those talk shows. Another was a famous film star, who was beginning to spiral down into the what-ever-happened-to pit. And some were obvious businessmen in their shiny Beamers and Benzes. I always turned up my TV volume when I was home during the day, to drown out the sound of her beat-downs, and the elated moans and groans of her constituents.

That spring, late one Wednesday morning, I was

walking back from the local farmer's market, carrying bags of ripe, organic, strawberries, un-husked sweet corn, a jar of honey and some fresh-baked whole grain bread. My doctor told me that with as stressful a job as I had, I would be wise to eat a healthier diet. Vodka was not on the list of approved sustenance, but I thought a nice, cool vodka slushy with the fresh, organic berries might be okay. Anyway, that would be lunch, along with a VCR cassette tape of *Invaders from Mars*, circa 1953.

The tape was in, the ingredients were just about to get tossed in the blender, and suddenly there was a knock at the door. It was Lady Brigette and she was in terrible trouble. It seemed one of her regular clients had passed out and she could not revive him.

"Call fucking 911! Are you kidding me?"

"No, please come over and see what you can do. I've tried everything and he's out cold! Please!"

Oh, well, I could hardly refuse, now could I? The last thing I wanted was for the police to come knocking at my door asking questions about a guy with a dildo up his ass, dead on the floor in the apartment next door.

"Okay, give me one minute." I closed the door, took out the tape, ate a handful of berries and washed them down with a swig of vodka.

~ ~ ~

I walked down the path to the front apartment and knocked on the door. Brigette had changed into something "less comfortable," and grabbed my hand as she led me into the second bedroom, made over into a dungeon-like lair, complete with hooks hanging from the ceiling, whips, chains, and various other "toys."

"I'll be damned!"

"You know this man?"

"Ah, me? No. Never saw him before in my life."

It was Mr. Ingersoll, splayed out on a mattress on the floor, his ankles attached to what Brigette, who was kind enough to educate me in the vernacular of her trade, informed me was a "spreader." His wrists were similarly affixed to another metal rod. Apparently he loved being hoisted upside down posed like Da Vinci's *Vetruvian Man* and paddled with a rather mean-looking prop that would make any Ivy League pledge bleat out "Please sir, may I have another!"

"You see," said Brigette pointing down to her captive client. "He's breathing, but I can't wake him up!"

"So, CPR is not required here. Have you tried smelling salts?" "

"Yes, I did, but that didn't work. What are we going to do?"

"We? **We** are not doing anything. You need to call for an ambulance."

"Please, you said you would help me."

Oh, gosh, what are neighbors for if not to aid in a time of obvious crisis?

"Did he take anything, pills, or anything?"

"I don't know. Usually, he's very alert, but today he came in kind of doped up or something."

Ah, yes. This was the day we lost the Patterson Payroll Account to our arch-nemesis, YS&W (Young, Sellers and Winston), or as I call them "Young, Smart and With-it."

"Have you checked his clothes?"

"Yes, but there is nothing."

I fished out his car keys from the pile of clothes on the floor and, having gotten his vintage red 1950 MG Roadster out of one tow yard or another, knew exactly what car to head for. It was only halfway up the block, on the opposite of the street. Sure enough, he had various bottles of this or that mind-numbing drug and a vial of coke, which I was tempted to pilfer, but thought better of it. I left the pharmacy in the car and hurried back to Lady Brigette, who was pacing back and forth, smoking one of those aromatic clove cigarettes in a peculiar finger-style holder I recognized from the movie *SUNSET BOULEVARD*.

"He took a downer, but as long as he is breathing, he should come to in a couple of hours. No problem."

"Oh, yes, there is a problem. I have other clients coming over today. One is a referral and it wouldn't do to turn him away. He could be good for other business. He's a famous director and makes lots of pictures. You'd know him, his name is ..."

"Ah, ah, ah, no, no, no. First rule of being a good Dominatrix is not to divulge any of the names of your clients. Plausible deniability and all. I'm sure you agree."

"Oh," she laughed. "I guess you are right. But what do I do with this one?"

"Here, I'll help you unshackle him and together we can drag him to your bedroom and just close the door until the other guys leave. Simple. Yes?"

The Babes who became Freddie Girls were right; he was impressively endowed and hairless as a newborn baby.

"Ahem ... do you mind if I ask you a question?" I said as I backed down the short hallway and into her bedroom carrying Mr. Ingersoll underneath his arms. Thank God he had a runner's body; slim, lean and built for speed.

"No. What?"

"How long has this one been coming here?"

"Oh, he's been a client for years. Before I moved here, he came to a little A-frame house I rented in the Hollywood hills. He's very sweet and funny, and always tips very generously. Why? I thought you said you didn't know him."

"No reason, just making conversation, I guess."

Mr. Ingersoll was sleeping peacefully on the bearskin rug on the side of Brigette's bed, covered with a white down comforter, his head resting on a goose down pillow. I bid my neighbor *adieu* just as her "Director" came through the front gate. I feigned tending to my potted plants just outside my front door, but managed to get a fleeting glimpse of him before he entered her apartment. I won't tell you who he was, but he was a major player in the entertainment industry.

A few minutes later, I heard the dulcet tones of *"Yes, YES, harder, HARDER. ACTION! CUT! PRINT"* Or whatever else a person in his line of work, who likes to be spanked, is apt to want to say.

He finally left and shortly thereafter so did our Sleeping Beauty.

I placed a call into the office to "check in," and asked The Sphinx if all was well. She said it was except Mr. Ingersoll was nowhere to be found and was late for a Creative Review with his team.

"Oh, I'm sure he'll be along shortly." And I left it at that; never telling anyone about my mission of mercy, or about Lady Brigette, or that Director, who shall remain nameless.

But that's a story for another day ...

Chapter 6

REQUIEM FOR AN AD MAN

For your listening pleasure: *"Super Freak" - Rick James*

Quote for the day: *"Take a look at this fucking request from the new guy and tell me ... can Armageddon be far behind?"*

*I*n the movie *Amadeus*, the character Salieri confronts God and accuses Him of instilling the talent he deserved into "a boastful, lustful, snotty, infantile boy." And even as he is caught up in his envious hatred for the genius Mozart, he admires him and ultimately kills him, but is punished by living and dying overshadowed by his greatness ... doomed for all of eternity to be merely mediocre.

This is exactly how most of the Creative staff at HIP, Inc. felt during the short but brilliant career of Quentin, *L'Enfant Terrible!*

"So what's the skinny on the new kid?" I asked The Sphinx, since hers is the only real opinion that counts here. The truth, the whole truth and nothing but the truth is what you will get from this Babe. Or at least as much of it as she thinks you can stomach.

"I'm guessing you will find out as soon as you open this

envelope," she said, handing one over with almost imperceptible handwriting that might have read "Office Services," or "Often 5 Vices" ... depending which way you turned it.

"Take a look at this fucking request from the new guy and tell me ... can Armageddon be far behind?"

The Sphinx took the note and smiled in her "Cheshire Cat" way. "What? I see nothing unusual here."

"Are you nuts? He's asking for, among other things, a built-in window seat, new white shag carpeting, black light paint on the walls, and a leather sofa. I'm only glad he didn't ask for a hot tub!"

His various furniture needs aside, after he settled in and as his many other demands were communicated and met, betting began in earnest among the Gents and Babes alike, as to how long this freak of creativity would actually last before his demise. Like all the betting pool sheets that passed through these hallowed halls, for every sporting event known to mankind, the "Kick the Bucket Pool" was no different, and jackpots, ranging from $100 to $1,000, filled up faster than last year's Super Bowl.

I bought three squares on the pool, "3 weeks," "8 months" and "October 19th", whichever came first. Meanwhile, Quentin was busy looking at the world through the eyes of a child ... Damien comes to mind, or Rosemary's Baby, or that Chucky kid, and he treated his office with the same care any teenage boy who was probably raised by parents so well passed the point of caring that all they could do is pray he moved out by age 18; and who lit candles in church to that hope, periodically shoving food under the door of a room they dare not enter. It would have been, to say it best, a candidate for one of the reality shows about hoarders. The once-new shag carpeting, what one could see of it, was no doubt host for some not yet discovered bio-warfare concoction. The walls covered with signs and posters from movies that must have somehow seeped into his ten-second-, thirty-second-, or sixty-second-geared consciousness long enough for him to be inspired at some level or another: "Road? Where we're going, we don't need roads," "Wax on. Wax off," "I know you are, but what am I?" and my personal favorite, "This one goes to eleven."

He often sat nearly upside down in his custom built boxed-in, cushioned window seat , his high-top black Keds scuffing up the window soffit, and his not-often-washed hair adding a petroleum-like sheen to both the glass and the fabric settee, pencil in mouth, when it, along with dozens of others, was not imbedded in the acoustic tile above his head.

He normally kept his door ajar ... not open, not closed ... always ajar. As if to invite a peek wherein he could use this as an excuse to stare rudely, get up from said Yoga-like repose, storm over to the door, expounding expletives, and then slam the door shut. Sometimes after these tizzy fits, his office neighbors could swear they heard him crying and we all began to refer to him as Lord of the Flies, or LOTF for short.

The only Babe who could remotely stand him, and stand up to him was Vivian, the newest in that Conga line of Freddie Girls. She had him tightly wrapped around her little finger, so much so that when she called him to Ingersoll's office for a chin-wag about his latest piece of work on the LadyGlow product, he practically shivered like a small designer pup. He worshiped her. *"Good boy, now speak!"* (And it better be good ... because the client is expecting to be blown away in tomorrow's Presentation by your so-called creative juices.)

~~~

"Because YOU know where that Special Spot is ... use **LADYGLOW***, and HE will too!"*

Long, very long moment of complete and utter silence ...

"Is that it?" asked the Client.

This was a make-or-break moment since all other attempts at pleasing them on this product had failed in a horrible, limp kind of way that made this presentation so vital to our self-esteem, self-respect and most important, to our bottom line. Displease a client once, well, everyone does that. Twice? Even twice you might be redeemed because of your other work for them. But a third time? And on a product that it was said was a personal favorite of the client's own wife, as in "Happy Wife, Happy Life."

No one moved an eyelash, or breathed, their sphincters tightening, visions of bankruptcy racing through their heads, resumes that were tucked away suddenly needed updating, and thoughts of "Who shall I call first, my wife, girlfriend, boyfriend, lover, bookie, dealer?" were rolling around the collective mind-set.

"I LOVE IT!"

Really. Really? Oh, well of course you do ...

Handshakes all around, slaps on the back and on the closest available butt, male and female ... and the call everyone waits for ... to me, TOM, for some champagne and munchies.

I have our local liquor store on speed dial and set to work to celebrate this victory. I call The Sphinx and the OS Team and the word spreads fast to meet in Conference Room Prime at 4:00 p.m. (I wonder if they will pass out free samples of the product?)

LOTF arrives to a packed room, hoisted up on a chair, carried by TPTB, wearing a makeshift laurel leaf wreath the Art Department made up at the last minute. He did his best to be modest, when Messrs. Ingersoll and Hamilton and Pride praised him for his talent, and for getting the client to commit to an entire campaign based on his new tag line.

A splendid time was had by all ... not to the extent of the usual shenanigans so prevalent at our rather notorious Christmas parties; we only had ten people who needed cab vouchers vs. forty or more, and no one got naked ... at least in the conference room, that we know of, but then there was that fleeting scene when the elevator opened up ... well, never mind.

And so began a long (by Adland standards) run of successful ads for our Sugar Daddy, Bread 'n Butter client P-B Industries. LadyGlow was a consumer hit at long last, second in sales only to Ramrod, the client's flagship product.

LOTF was even asked to write a PSA (Public Service Announcement for those of you who don't speak Adlandese), in keeping with the famous "Your Brain on Drugs" campaign. His ad showed an obviously strung out female and in other ads a gent looking at themselves in a mirror in a bathroom where the counter was strewn with drug paraphernalia ..."All coked up and nowhere to go?" asked the voiceover. It was sponsored by a rehab facility that, of all people, Elliott Monroe was working for as a consultant ... and who better, I ask you?

Damn if it didn't win a Cleo ... and a Belding ... the Adland equivalents of the Oscar and the Emmy.

He was poised to move into a corner office, with all the *accoutrement* that goes with one. And then it happened ... the scourge of every creative personality ... but most particularly copywriters ... the dreaded "Writer's Block!"

The client was less than enthusiastic about LOTF's next offering ... I'm sure Mr. Ingersoll paid a visit to Lady Brigette after that meeting ... and the next ad didn't even make it outside Mr. Ingersoll's office, but was left on the floor along with the pile of other less than stellar ideas, which the newest Freddie Girl, Eva, gathered up and shredded, one sheet at a time, to the terror of all the creatives within earshot.

The following month, the same thing happened ... crickets ...

And then faint rumblings from the client amounting to the hideous phrases, "What have you done for me lately?" and "Exactly how much am I paying you?"

LOTF was doomed ... and I was still in the running with a square that said "October 19th."

~~~

When someone leaves Adland it's kind of like a yard sale sign goes up on their office door. Fellow Adlanders come in by stealth, and remove wanted items or "trade up" to, for example, a better chair, leaving their chair in its place. (But no one removes the leather sofa lest they wish to incur *The Wrath of TOM*.)

I had a HAZMAT crew come in and clean the office; tearing out the carpeting, repainting the walls, replacing all the work-surfaces that couldn't be cleaned and that didn't have something carved into them. The sofa was sent out for professional fumigation. One of the Babes offered to burn some sage.

~~~

Alas, I didn't win the Kick the Bucket Pool. Prizes went to a fellow Creative, one of my OS Team associates, and Mr. Pride (!) And as for LOTF, he now lives in Wyoming in a small town, running a tavern, where he has been known to get drunk and sing Karaoke, and tell tall tales of when he was a Creative, *par excellence.*

But that's a story for another day ...

Chapter 7

MY MORIARTY

For your listening pleasure: *"Money for Nothing"* - Dire *Straits*

Quote for the day: *"There's something very hinky going on here."*

As TOM, part of my role is to lead my Office Services troop in the daily battle of maintaining the office space and operations here at HIP, Inc. Each OSP (Office Services Professional) has their own task, and yet each one is able, on a moment's notice, to take over for any other person on the team. Cross-training is a key element to keeping the staff happy and productive because they aren't worried about the million and one things we are in charge of – space, furniture, HVAC, mail and shipping, copy, fax and binding processes, conference room set-ups, catering, coffee stations, office supplies, décor, plants, flowers, parking, safety, housekeeping (especially keeping Attila dusted off,) security, etc., etc., etc. We are the selfless, thankless (sometimes,) hands behind the scenes that keep the ship operational while the crew goes on shore leave.

We have only one rule, borrowed from *The Godfather*: "Never take sides against the family." We swear to come to each others aid, no matter what, and while we share all the details of each and every event, story, scandal, news-bite, whatever, that happens in this agency or in Adland at large, we also promise we will go to our deaths or unemployment (whichever comes first) before we squeal to an outsider. Naturally, that is why no one who is written about in this book barely resembles any actual person, living or dead, and all names, events or locales have been changed to protect ... well, everyone!

As to my OS team, it was a honor to work with each and every one of them, and this story is dedicated to them.

~~~

"Tom, there is a police officer here to see you," said The Sphinx.

"Swell. I'll be right down." I hung up. "Oh, God, the jig's up!" Having once led a life full of riotous adventures, there's no telling what the fuck this was about.

"Hi, I'm TOM, how may I help?" I extended my hand and received a firm handshake from a man who could have been sent from Central Casting: "Wanted – All American, clean-shaven, well-built, Caucasian male, roughly 6 feet, 185 lbs. Eyes: Blue. Hair: Dirty Blonde. Early '80s Robert Redford-type smile, should audition wearing button-down white shirt, no tie, tan Dockers and brown loafers."

"Hello. I'm Detective Jordan Finch. Is there somewhere private we can talk?"

"Huh?" I said, trying to get *The Way We Were* out of my mind. "I'm sorry ... yes, let's step into the Conference Room right here."

Conference Room Beta, with its mid-20th century flair, was the perfect surroundings for him as he sat on the ottoman of the black leather Eames Lounge Chair, leaning towards me as I sat on the white leather Bantam sofa. It was obvious he didn't know how good-looking he really was. "How can that be?" I thought. "Maybe he's got a touch of Body Dysmorphic Syndrome, or something?" I tried not to look him straight in the eyes, and searched my pockets for a business card as he presented his:

Detective Jordan Finch, XYZ Police Department, Fraud and Bunco Division, etc., etc.

"Hmmmm? You're out of your jurisdiction, aren't you?" I mentioned this because HIP, Inc. was located in a separate municipality surrounded by a much larger one.

"Well," he laughed (disarmingly, I might add.) "You're right, but I do have permission from this jurisdiction and my commanding officer to follow the case I'm working on to wherever it leads me."

"Here? This case of yours leads you here ... to me?" (Well, ain't that a bitch. I'm going to be arrested by someone I'd pay money to sleep with.)

"Yes, I'm told you are in charge of Office Services? You are the ..." He opened up one of those little notebooks and began to flip the pages.

"The Office Mom."

"Yes, that's right. And the office copiers would fall under your authority?"

"I guess you could say that. Actually, they fall under the 'authority,' as it were, of one of my OPS, Willamina. Why? And by the way, would you like some coffee? Water, perhaps?" I'd surmised that no arrest was pending ... Whew!

"No, but thank you." (Please smile again ... please,

please, PLEASE.) "The case involves the counterfeiting of AMEX Travelers Cheques. We've discovered quite a large ring of thieves concentrated in this part of the county, and have made several arrests already. Evidence from the crimes show us the phony documents were made on one of five color copiers, all owned by HIP, Inc., at this address."

"Do tell? How do you know they were made on our machines, if you don't mind me asking?"

"Well, I will need your complete cooperation—" (you got it, Honey) "—while I work this out, and so I will fill you in on a little known secret in the copy industry." He leaned in a little as if he were going to whisper. "As a precaution against this very thing, that is, making copies of legitimate documents such as checks, money, bank notes, etc., for reasons of theft or fraud, the manufacturers devised a way of imprinting a code on each page that is copied which can be read and checked against all sales information about all the different types of manufacturers and the various equipment they produce. It was really quite simple for us to take the false document and trace the code to this company as having been the last purchaser of these machines."

"And you think one of my staff members is busy making these traveler's checks? And then what?"

"Oh, I don't know for sure who is making them. That's part of the investigation. It could be someone from the cleaning crew or a vendor who has reason to be in your copy areas, or even your Security Guard. I noticed there was a young man in your first floor lobby at the desk there." Again he referred to his little notebook. "Name is Kaleb, spelled with a 'K.' His accent tells me he is Jamaican?"

"Yes, that's correct. He's a very sweet kid...personable

and well-liked here."

"How long has he worked here?"

"About eight months. He's the third guard we've had from the service. The other two just didn't work out."

"Why is that?"

"Well, as you might guess, ad agencies are a different breed than, say, a law firm or a manufacturer. We're more like a retailer ... the customer is always right ... even when they're wrong. So we needed someone who looked the part but isn't too gung-ho about actually going so far as to wrestle someone to the floor and handcuff them ... you know?"

"Yes, I think I understand. What are his hours? And is he the only guard on duty?" He took notes while I spoke.

"He works Tuesday through Sunday, 3:00 p.m. until midnight, that's when the garage downstairs closes and the building is locked up. At five p.m., they open the garage up for general parking and because the public passes through the lobby to exit out onto the street, we have a guard to keep people from trying to go upstairs to any of our floors. If he is out sick, the service sends someone else to cover for him, usually a supervisor, but we haven't had that happen for quite a while."

"And Mondays?"

"The building and the garage both close at 6 o'clock.

"Okay, so he works six days a week, and what time do the majority of your employees leave the building?"

"Depends. Account Services, Media, Traffic, Finance, HR keep fairly normal hours (if you can call anything in Adland normal,) and Creative, Production, they can work all night sometimes to meet deadlines. Sometimes the

Creatives leave work early and then come back after hours to work, undisturbed."

"Would you have a list of these staff members?"

"Not really, and I couldn't give you that information anyway. You'd have to talk to HR and get them to give you a list."

"Well, I don't really think that's necessary. I already have a good idea who is making the copies. I just need a way to prove it. So does your security guard have access to the space after hours?"

"Yes, of course, part of his job is to walk the space with the cleaning crew supervisor when the crew arrives and then again when they leave."

"What company do you use and could I have the name of the supervisor?"

"Sure. I'll have to go to my office and I'll print out the information for you."

"Great. May I see where all these machines are?" He showed me a list of the equipment he wanted to see.

"Of course. The first one is on this floor, in the Copy Center. Follow me."

I gave him an impromptu tour of the first floor and he asked if he could have copies of the floor plans, which I said I'd be happy to provide.

We walked into the Copy Center and I introduced him to Willamina, who later told me she thought he was "soooo fine, and too bad he was with law enforcement." She is one of those rare employees who is a triple-hitter; imaginative, hardworking and excellent at what she does, enjoying every moment of being at HIP, Inc. She often jokes that they will have to carry her out on a stretcher because she is never leaving on her own. As long as there is a HIP, Inc., she will be here to manage the Copy Center and any other assignment they want to give her. Like The Sphinx, she was also a purveyor of common-sense advice and a friend.

"You really think someone here is making these copies? On my machines? Oh, no, sir, no. NO."

Jordan remarked that she seemed a little miffed that someone would be using the equipment for such a nefarious scheme.

"Oh, it's not that...it's just that most of them are too distracted to figure out how to do it. You see, you'd have to line up the front and back master just so to get the product to come out exactly right and be expert at cutting the paper. To begin with you'd have to know how to the load the paper, and make adjustments for what I'm guessing is a special type of paper. And most of these people don't know enough to make a regular copy, let alone what you're suggesting."

"She's right, you know. If it weren't for the Babes and Willamina here, nothing would get printed in this place."

"Nothing you'd want the client to see, anyway. I take the shit-pile of papers they bring me and turn it into 'sugar'"

"So other than you and maybe a handful of staff, no one in this agency could make such copies?"

"No, I don't think so ... say, you're not accusing her, I hope?"

"No, not at all, she checks out already. We did a preliminary investigation and have come up with only one suspect."

"Really, who is it?" we both asked.

"Kaleb, your security guard."

"That kid? Ah, no. He's dumber than he looks and

believe me, that's dumb."

"I'm going to kill him ... messing with my machines!"

"Now, ladies, let's not get too riled up. Wouldn't you rather catch him in the act and solve this crime with me?"

"Sure, why not. I love a good crime story."

"Is there a reward?" asked Willamina.

"Yes, what about that?"

"No. I'm afraid not. The only reward is knowing that you've helped solve one of the largest counterfeiting rings operating out of this city, and one that may be tied to a nationwide operation."

"Oh, well ... sure."

"Seems to me there should be a reward somewhere," Willamina said, shaking her head.

The game was afoot, and we began to formulate a plan...

~~~

"Give this envelope to "You Know Who," and thanks for the loan," said Mr. Pride, sliding a pair of handcuffs and a manila envelope towards Kaleb, who slipped both into his top desk drawer with ease.

"No problem, sir. Anytime."

Mr. Pride waited silently and got into the next elevator headed to the garage. His wife, Charity (who really didn't know the meaning of the word,) had yet another inane fundraiser dinner she wanted him to attend with her ... Save The Something or other. He knew Kaleb would see that the envelope and the cash it contained would get to the intended party. He just didn't want to cross paths with that person, outside certain circles, if it could be helped. Furthermore, he knew Kaleb would "tip" himself. That was to be expected, he thought, and always put in an extra

Franklin for said reason. His classic 1976 black Mercedes 450SL convertible roared out of the garage, Blaupunkt cranked up, Steely Dan's "Hey Nineteen" playing. The whole thing could have been the opening scene from a soft-core porno and he was running late.

~~~

Kaleb had two things on his mind. One being the cop who went upstairs. (See, I told you the gossip grapevine was quick at HIP, Inc.) And the other was taking the first bill in the envelope off the top for himself. He was sure "You Know Who" would not notice and Mr. Pride never said anything. Anyway, he was providing a service and thought he should get a little something. Call it rent on the handcuffs. He gave them a sniff. They smelled like S-E-X and tears.

"Good afternoon, sir," said Kaleb, taking the Visitor's badge from Jordan who had just exited from the elevator vestibule.

"Thank you ... Kaleb, is it?"

"Yes, sir. Thank you, sir."

"I'll be seeing you," said Jordan, giving him a quick cross between a wave and a salute as he exited the front door of the building and disappeared into the din and bodies of the crowd on the boulevard.

"There's something very hinky going on around here," thought Jordan, having furtively witnessed the exchange between Mr. Pride and the dumb, "like a fox," Kaleb. He would get his "Moriarty" if it was the last thing he did, and no one was going to stand in the way of this pinch.

Kaleb sat back in his chair and wondered what other surprises might be in store tonight.

~~~

Jonathan Pride, or "JP" as he was known in Adland, was as foul a creature as ever walked the halls of any company, much less an ad agency, where good looks don't hurt one darn bit. He was short and bald and fat, with uneven features. Fate had dealt him a cruel hand when it came to looks, and his personality was equally vile, having suffered through childhood, adolescence and early adulthood from the disdain others could not help but show him. But worse was the pity that crossed their faces, as if looking upon a circus freak. He was, for all intents and purposes, the *Rumplestilskin of Adland*. Fortunately, for him, he really could spin straw into gold, in much the same way as his mythical doppelganger.

When it came to money – making it, investing it, multiplying it like rabbits going at it from dusk until dawn, for himself and those he worked for – he was an absofuckinglutely goddamn, certifiable genius. He had the Midas touch and even when he was getting or giving a hand job, he thought about only one thing – cold, hard, cash. Whether it was dollars, pounds, yen or gold, the thought of money and how to get it and make it grow consumed his every waking and sleeping moment. He did not need to count sheep; he merely closed his eyes and saw the NYSE ticker tape display and that was enough to send him into dreamland.

He loved money more than he loved anything or anyone else, and it was this love of money which caused him to seethe with a terrible ache at having to write checks for his wife's endless charitable indulgences. Tonight was no exception, and he felt a small comfort at knowing he was only out ten grand to help save the ... uh ... whatever.

Actually, the act of writing the check was his favorite part, and he did it with such flourish, one would think he didn't mind parting with the money it represented. And that was because he had a special pen just for the occasion; a custom-made Montblanc 18K gold and diamond tipped pen. It cost $33,000.

Yes, you read it here, folks. He was signing a check to a charitable organization with a pen that cost far more than the value of the check he was writing. And he loved every moment of it. It was almost better than S-E-X ... almost. Maybe his wife would take pleasure in seeing his generosity and maybe she would, in turn, be generous when they got home. He hoped so. The truth was, the one thing he wanted most in the entire world, was to feel deep down in his soul that she loved him for more than his money. Funny thing was, while she could spend it faster than the US Treasury could print it, "JP," in his own twisted way, admired her for that talent.

One check he did not mind writing at all was the monthly stipend he gave You Know Who. Mind you, he was not so crass as to leave money on her nightstand. (He tried that once in the beginning and let's just say it did not go over very well.) But rather, as time went by, paid, out of an account he opened under a variation of his real name, all her bills and credit cards and the mortgage on her condo overlooking the ocean, which he chose because he liked the view and the fact that the parking lot entrance was on a quiet side street with little traffic. He leased her car as one of his own afforded to him by HIP, Inc., and made sure she was as happy as any, dare I say it, mistress could ever be.

"Happy wife, happy life." Happy mistress, great S-E-X.

Only, poor thing, she didn't think of herself as a mistress, and since she no longer worked in Adland could no longer be counted as one of the Babes. Actually, she never was a Babe, more of a Wanna-be-Babe. You can always tell who they are. Gals who look amazing, like some fashion model, on the days when their paramour is in the office, and a veritable bag lady, sans makeup, wearing the sweats they worked out in that morning, when he is out of town or home sick, or wherever. Sometimes, early in these relationships (during the ARP, or Acute Romantic Period) she will travel with him, and depending on his situation with his wife, it will be a clandestine operation or brazenly out in the open.

Anyway, Illegally Blonde, for example, before or after her promotion, would never be caught dead without what she referred to as her battle armor; polished in dress, hair and make-up, always looking stunning, and turned her nose up those who didn't when their lovers were absent.

"I know it sounds a bit uppity, but I would neva' dare come here lookin' like somethin' the cat draaagged in." She'd say in that somewhere in the fly-over-states drawl of hers, which had a tendency to surface after a typical Adland three-drink minimum lunch.

If you ever saw *Breakfast At Tiffany's* (and if you haven't – gasp! – I don't want to know), you know the character Mag Wildwood, played by Dorothy Whitney, who at 5'11" was a tall glass of bourbon and had a simply marvelous Appalachian-meets-Manhattan accent? Well, Illegally Blonde was the perfect blend of this character and the one and only Marilyn, and had something to say on any subject that involved involvement with an M-A-L-E.

Now there's a subject every Babe knows something about ... M-A-L-E-S; not guys or dudes, or pals, or Gents, or even just men in the general sense of the word, but bona fide, hard-drinking, chain-smoking, cuss-happy, 6-pack abs and all their hair, "Yes, I am hot stuff, Honey," type of bad boy that every woman fantasizes about but never admits to because doing so would make us as Neanderthal as they can be, and was exactly the type of guy Illegally Blonde grew up with in the little one-street town she was from.

~~~

"Good afternoon, Kaleb," said Jordan. He was carrying a large briefcase. "I'm here to see TOM and I'm expected."

"Here you are, sir," said Kaleb, giving Jordan a Visitor's badge. "May I help you with that case?"

"No, that's fine. I've got it. Thanks, anyway."

"Yes, sir. Thank you, sir." Kaleb eyed the case out of the corner of his eye as Jordan entered the elevator.

"Hi, Kaleb," said Vicki and Elaine, arm-in-arm, coming back from a meeting with the client. "Everything okay?"

"Oh, yes. Things just fine." Or were they ...

~~~

"I've brought the cameras we talked about," said Jordan, taking two black binders out of his case, and laying them on the worktable in the Copy Center. (Please remember, this was long before the days of nanny cams with cameras so small several can practically dance on the head of a pin, cannot be "remote controlled," and only have a one-angle view of what is going on.) We set them up at two of the five color copiers we have spread out in HIP, Inc., planning to rotate them weekly, and with Kaleb Kam in place, all that was left to do was hurry up and wait.

The first weekend went by and the results were dismal, not unlike today's ghost/monster hunting shows where they don't ever seem to really capture anything, much less a ghost or a Yeti.

Second weekend, same thing.

Third weekend, ditto.

By the fourth week, I'd given Jordan his own workstation and suddenly every Babe in the place wanted to know who my new OS Assistant was, and was he single and was he straight.

"He's not my assistant; he's a vendor. I don't know," (really, I never asked because my entire fantasy life at that point would have died a tragic death.) "And, I'm fucking counting on it."

"He's gay," deadpanned The Sphinx. "Don't ask me how I know."

Early that next Friday, Jordan told us that recent information indicated that our cameras were placed by the wrong machines and we'd have to move them. (You recall that a code is invisibly imprinted on every color copy ... I'm guessing more bogus cheques had been cashed since this whole thing began.)

Week five, again, no results, Jordan got a nameplate and personalized notepads.

Week six, we finally caught a glimpse of a hand placing a cut-and-paste original on the glass of the unit in Creative, but since the image was in B/W, you couldn't tell if the person (maybe man, or a woman with very large hands) was white or black, or just someone with a dark tan, or what the image was exactly, only that it looked kind of like a series of images ganged on a single sheet, and they may have been the items in question or the Sunday comics.

"This is going well, is it?" I asked Finch. (Don't leave, please don't leave.)

"Yeah, this sucks. I kind of thought we'd a caught him by now. Are you sure it's Kaleb?" Willamina said as she left a plate of blueberry muffins, fruit and a cut of coffee on his desk. "Leftovers from a meeting in Conference Room Beta, courtesy of the Babes in Traffic."

"Thank you!" he said, and flashed that smile. (Oh my God, don't leave.) "Yes, I still think so, but my superior is getting a lot of heat on this case, and he's already threatened to pull the plug on this whole operation so we only have one more week, but we do have information from our forensic unit that all the most recent checks have been made from the machines on your Creative Department floor, so I'll concentrate my efforts there."

"Well, Willamina and I have been talking about this, and we have a plan."

"Yeah, if the cameras can't catch him in the act, we will nab him ourselves!"

"Now, ladies ..."

Our plan was simple. Two cameras would be placed on the other floors, just in case, and the three of us would lie in wait in offices adjacent to the copiers on the suspect floor; Willamina and I having strict instructions merely to observe and not attempt even a "citizens arrest." If Finch caught him, great; if we saw Kaleb in the room with the copier then we could at least report that and the authorities would take it from there.

It was just past midnight, and I had fallen asleep on the sofa of one of the Art Directors, waking suddenly to the sound of someone singing! Nervous, but curious, I peeked through the cracked door only to see LOTF (obviously, this was prior to his departure from Adland), staggering down the hall, singing the jingle from one of his latest ads. He must have been plastered, because he threw up in a nearby trashcan, lurched into his own office and slammed the door. The next thing I heard was Jordan yelling, "Stop! Drop your bags! Get your hands up!" Willamina came rushing down the hall and we both turned the corner to see Detective Finch and Kaleb, each holstering their weapons and handcuffing two teenage males. Their backpacks were stuffed with stacks of the illicit merchandise.

"Nice work." Willamina said, with admiration, as she peered at one of the copies.

"You're under arrest for counterfeiting. You have the right to remain silent ..."

And so it was that Kaleb had been the hero and not the perp after all. A few weeks before, on his regular nightly rounds, he had seen the boys on the Creative Department floor enter a stairwell that led up from the garage. He wasn't sure if they were relatives or friends of a staff member, so he didn't say or do anything about it at the time. The night of the big take down, while checking out the garage, he noticed one of the stairwell doors had been propped open, and heard the sound of singing coming from an upper floor. He followed the sound, and saw the boys, carrying backpacks, enter one of the three copy rooms. Before he could walk in, he was intercepted by Detective Finch, who quickly filled him in on what was happening, and they both were in on the bust.

That Monday, it was all over the agency and Kaleb

received a nice bonus check and sincere thanks from Mr. Hamilton. Jordan thanked Willamina and me, and packed up his two cameras. The whole OS Department and several of the Babes gave him an impromptu goodbye party, with cake and everything. A couple of them also gave him their home numbers and a flirty invitation to "get together sometime." As far as I know, none of them ever heard from him, so either he was the consummate professional, or The Sphinx was right. (It was all I could do not to swipe the hair from his forehead, and instead gave him a firm handshake and an almost tearful goodbye.)

One week later, Kaleb was promoted to supervisor at his company and another security guard, Tony, took his place at our building. JP's handcuff connection was no more, although someone did report seeing him at The Pleasure Chest in West Hollywood buying some, accompanied by a Babe who was not Mrs. JP, and who, from the description, was not "You Know Who" either.

One month later, there was a brief news article about a Fagin-like counterfeiting mastermind who used teenage boys to print and pass fake AMEX Traveler's Cheques. They gave special mention to Detective Jordan Finch. Alas, no picture. It wouldn't have done him justice, anyway.

But that's a story for another day ...

Chapter 8

THE STORY OF MR. "O"

For your listening pleasure: *"Mr. Roboto" - Styx*

Quote for the day: *"I don't ask questions. I just take their money and use it for things that really interest me."*

*R*ob Osborne was the ultimate temp.
In Adland where everyone sells their heart and soul, and often their body, and sometimes promises their first born, to work in an agency on any account or at any job no matter what it might be, he had one of the best damn jobs in the agency.

He worked for one person, in this case, Mr. Pride, and did not have to work on any client business. He only worked on what was of concern to our financial guru ... business or personal.

If anyone else were to get a call, he was a gentleman and wrote down the date, time and a call back number ... nothing else ... absolutely no details ... ever.

Now you might not think this would be a problem, but please remember, this was "back in the day," long before we were all wired in the Cloud and if there was an emergency, so sorry. Until you got that little slip of paper, and made the return call, you were screwed and could not get a head start on anything. Even if you called in for messages, he gave nary a detail, and he was so nice about it, no one ever had a bad word to say. He was his own entity. Pure. Savant. Untouchable. We called him "RoBO/TEMP." ("Rob O.........Temp" is how it read on the phone list and he named himself this before the movie of a similar name came out ... just sayin'.)

Still, that "RoBO/TEMP" deemed you worthy to even take a message was a point of pride for anyone who was so favored.

He had a very cultured way of speaking – real English – like the actors in B/W movies...George Sanders comes to mind, who once said of himself, honestly, *"I don't ask questions. I just take their money and use it for things that really interest me."*

He had been on stage on Broadway ... a chorus-line dandy; and later did the same thing in those big-budget 1940's Hollywood musicals directed by Busby Berkeley. He was probably much older than anyone thought, but he was tall and slender and had the vigor of youth. He dressed in a classic style; grey or black slacks, black loafers, a dress shirt with the sleeves neatly rolled back, a simple tank-style watch, and had meticulous grooming. He had a twin brother who was rumored to have sailed off to Pape'ete in the '60s, and was never seen again, although he did send the infrequent postcard of scantily clad native girls, beckoning his brother to join him.

"My brother is the wild one ... I, on the other hand, thrive on the calm, collected nature of a schedule. I eat the same thing, wear the same thing and do the same thing. I have peace, you see ... blessed peace."

Well, that's what he told us, anyway; but here's the truth ...

"Another glass of champagne, Mr. O?" asked the flight attendant. "The Captain wanted me to tell you we have clear skies and minimal crosswinds, so we are on schedule for a smooth flight into McCarran this afternoon."

For those of you who don't know, McCarran International Airport is in Las Vegas, or Sin City, or Lost Wages, or any of a number of nicknames that belong to one hell of a party town a mere 45 minutes of flight time from LAX. And if you are maybe not quite a Whale, but definitely a High Roller, a casino will indeed fly you out on their Lear jet and offer accommodations, drinks, fine dining and entertainment, all for the privilege of taking your money at cards, craps or whatever was your pleasure. The limo arrived and squired Mr. O to the hotel, which will remain nameless, and he was greeted by the driver and the valet and the bellman, and the front desk, and even the floor maid who was passing. They would all nod, or doff their caps, they knew him, he was a valuable guest and a very generous tipper.

Now one might ask how it was that someone who worked as a temp for the nearly poverty-level wages of a clerical worker in Adland would have enough to be courted as a well-heeled visitor to the West Coast gambling Mecca of the free world? Embezzlement, perhaps? Blackmail? (Certainly a possibility in Adland, as you know by now.) A periodic trust fund disbursement?

Nah.

He worked, and worked, and worked, and worked. Living a life so absent of even the most moderate of creature comforts, and so devoid of companionship, a monk would find it hard to live in it ...a small rent-controlled studio apartment (though the view was lovely), no car (always walked or took the bus,) no eating out (or in sometimes for that matter,) no phone, no cable ... hell, no TV (!), no "stuff" to weigh him down or to insure, no pets, no women (or men for that matter.)

And he saved and saved and saved, and saved, until he had cash enough to make a yearly escape to Vegas to transform from the nonthreatening "RoBO/Temp" into "Mr. O," *bon vivant man about town*, where he would hobnob with his fellow gamblers and men of risk and adventure for a week or two or three depending on if Lady Luck was in his corner or not. He would then withdraw to a modest hotel off the Strip and spend the rest of the season by the pool soaking up the sun, and hitting the $5 buffets at the less prestigious hotels where no one would know who he was in either his fantasy or real life.

He never worried about "matter/anti-matter" meeting in the same universe. In Vegas you either have money or you don't, subsequently you either count or you don't and no one ever suspected that a person as seemingly benign as he would dare to cross the chasm that separated the two.

He would return to Adland, usually in a month or two, by which time Mr. Pride had fired or caused to flee at least 4 or 5 replacements, only to utter an audible sigh of relief when Human Remains would notify him that "RobO/Temp" had called up to see if there were any new assignments.

And then one year, he did not return.

Mr. Pride wept.

The Babes cried.

There was a general sadness and the spasmodic wailing and gnashing of teeth, mostly from Mr. Pride.

I thought about getting drunk ... but couldn't afford another round of rehab.

Only The Sphinx kept a calm head and said she had a "feeling" we would hear from him at some point.

Try as they might, HR could not get a hold of him and the letters they sent to his PO Box came back as "Undeliverable. No Forwarding Address."

And then one day, the following Spring, a small package arrived for Mr. Pride. It was a small snow globe ... from Las Vegas ... showing the hotels on The Strip ... and the snowflakes were dollar signs.

There was a note enclosed. Mr. Pride remained tight-lipped, except to tell us "RobO/TEMP" would not be returning, and he understood his reason completely.

Now some may say he hit the jackpot and lives in Vegas to this day, and one of the ad execs, whilst on vacation, swore they saw him walking down Fremont Street early one morning, eating a Danish and sipping coffee from a paper cup. Others muse that he met someone (a showgirl, perhaps) and the two had decided to settle down to a more conventional life in a small midwestern town after winning big.

All I know is we nominated him an Honorary Babe, and we will never forget him and miss him still.

But that's a story for another day ...

Chapter 9

PROMISES, PROMISES

For your listening pleasure: *"Crazy for You" - Madonna*

Quote for the day: *"Fuck you and good luck!"*

"*B*ehind every great man, is a greater Babe."
I know I am paraphrasing, and I don't know who wrote the original version of this, but I know that it is more often true than not. Years into my tenure at HIP, Inc., I ran into a sincerely nice Babe who was married to a man named Moe. Because the last name was so distinctive, I was certain she was the spouse of a man I will have always referred to as Angry Moe.

During my time in Adland, I worked with several Gents named Joe, Bob, Jim, Jerry, several Chucks and one or two Tims. Only one Moe, who made his own kind of Adland history in this story about what really happens behind the scenes of the slick and polished performance that is called a New Business Pitch or Presentation where the agency delivers their best promises to a potential new client.

I called him Angry Moe, though his nickname should have been "Fuck you!" since he said it about 1,000 times a day, and flipped off any and everybody who made him mad, which could be just about anybody. I remember his birthday cards, cakes and gifts all were emblazoned with this phrase. He loved it. I suppose he thought it was part of his "charm." He was not allowed, no surprise here, to have any direct contact with any of the clients whose business he worked on. He was a brilliant artist, however, and could deliver art direction on a dime, which is what Adland is all about in truth ... business, and not art, per se.

He was, at my first agency gig, a lower-level Assistant Art Director, whose cubicle walls were covered top-to-bottom and side-to-side with pictures, from ad shoots, *Playboy*, art house and motorcycle-garage-worthy calendars of women in various positions and stages of undress. No one cared, naturally, because this is Adland, after all, and if you blinked as you walked by the long row of cubicles in the land where all the other lower-level Assistant Whatevers sat, you might just miss it.

And then it happened. We were going to pitch a new client, who, as part of their visit, requested to take a tour of the agency. *Quelle horreur!*

The client was Japanese. It was for a motorcycle account that was destined to change the future of motorcycles in America. Because we didn't have much of a New Business pitch budget and were up against three other major Players in Adland reputed to have very sizable budgets, we didn't lift a finger to prepare for the pitch until about one week before they were to arrive. Then all Hell broke loose and there were the promised all-nighters, and endless lunch meetings, and powwows with TPTB and decisions about which Creatives would work on the pitch and which Account Executives should be assigned to the Account Group, just in case we actually scored this bird.

And as with all shit that hits the fan ... it hit me.

"TOM, you need to go down to Moe's cubicle and tell him to take down all his pictures. And don't let him intimidate you; just keep repeating 'you need to take down the pictures, you need to take down the pictures, you need to take down the pictures,'" my Boss-Lady Babe said, in full-blown "est" mode.

"Yeah, right, that's going to go over well. He would just as soon kill me!" I thought. "At the very least, his tirade of "Fuck you's" will probably make me cry." (God, I was such a sensitive Tot then ...)

"And don't let him tell you he'll get around to it. It's your responsibility to see that it's cleaned up before the client arrives."

I did my duty and went to see Moe, who, when he saw me, figured out immediately why I was there.

"Moe, I hope I'm not disturbing you ..." He just ignored me.

"But, you know that New Business pitch on Friday?" (The one you are **not** working on?) Well, the client wants to take a tour of the agency, and I've been asked to tell you ..."

"Fuck you!"

"Now, Moe, this isn't my idea, so please don't ..."

"Fuck you!" He added an over-the-shoulder one-finger gesture.

"Yes, but ..."

"Fuck you!" He's standing up ...

"Moe ... I know how this ..."

"Fuck you! Now get out! Get the fuck out of my face!"

You can only imagine how scared I was ... it was well known he was certifiable though would not be at this agency or any place in Adland were he not a gifted, solid, albeit at present, low-level Assistant Art Director. That coupled with his size, which was formidable to most men, let alone me – all five feet of me – and the fact that he sported a full beard and had bushy black, unkempt hair, along with a kind of wild-eyed look matching the Neanderthal model you see at the natural history museum displays of early man, made me momentarily rethink my budding career in Adland.

He was at the opening of his cubicle, as I stood on the hallway side of the imaginary "doorway" line, and I could feel all the other Assistant Whatevers holding their breath, listening intently, or quickly gathering up some paperwork and heading to a very early lunch so as not to get caught in the fray.

He was glaring at me as he lifted his middle finger once more in my face. "I'm **not** taking down my pictures ... I don't give a flying rat's **ass** about this stupid client ... I don't care **who** told you to come here ... if TPTB want to fire me, then **fuck** them, too!"

I gulped. Hard.

I thought about what my Boss-Lady Babe would do, and decided against repeating myself; and then wondered if I could ask to borrow one of her father's paid assassins to help, but then that whole story about her family's Mafia connection was probably still just a rumor.

Fact is, I was too scared to move. And he wasn't moving either. We stood face (mine) to chest (his) for a moment and then I turned and walked down the hall, hoping he wouldn't resort to throwing anything at me ... like a stapler or a letter opener. My face was hot and flush and I was doing everything I could not to burst into tears.

I got past the long Assistant Whatevers length of cubicles and was about to turn towards the Administrative and Account Services end of the floor, when I got mad. Not just a little mad, but fired-up, absolutely angry.

"How dare this asshole talk to me that way. Who the fuck does he think he is, anyway? This was a simple request on behalf of the agency, for Christ's sake. It might mean more money down the road for all of us. Not to mention the prestige of winning this account that three other major and much larger agencies were also pitching. Well, it would serve him right if I turned around and stomped back over to his cubicle in The Land of Assistant Whatevers and gave him a piece of my mind."

Yeah, right. I was no fool; I went back to my lovely Boss-Lady Babe and told her the whole story. She wasted no time going over to Moe's cubicle and promptly returned, getting on the phone to her boss, who went over to Moe's cubicle, and so on, right on up the agency food chain to the Executive VP, Creative Director who told the person who called him to "Fuck off … he may be an Assistant Art Director now, but I've got big plans for that guy!" And then he called my Boss-Lady Babe who looked at me and gave out a heavy sigh, before she put her forehead up and down a few times on her desk. (I'm guessing her next call was to sign up for another "est" graduate course.)

In the coming days, other Assistant Whatevers tried to "appease" Moe into relenting. They began to throw, into his cubicle, sheets of paper on which was written, printed or typed, some even with glued-on letters from cut-up news or magazine print, the words "Fuck You!" He read them and then crumpled them, and then tossed them on the floor. Pretty soon the pile on the carpet was about three feet deep. Still, he would not budge.

I guess they, too, wanted the account so they could get a stab at maybe getting their hands on this nifty little item of New Business and perhaps get out of The Land of Assistant Whatevers. Like I said, it was for a motorcycle account and had every chance of really making a difference to our bottom-line billing, and giving us a much-needed shot in the arm … we'd recently dropped from an A- rating to a B- in the Adland tabloids. Though our stable of clients was highly regarded, the two largest clients we had were regional West Coast, and this bird was national … big bucks. Still we all knew it was probably not going to be a win; but they had asked us to the dance and we couldn't say no.

As of Thursday night, the pictures and the pile were still there. I heard that plans were being made to ambush the cubicle early in the morning, but then Moe did something no one expected. He swept out the cubicle, leaving a flurry of paper balls in the hallway, brought in a cot and a portable TV, and covered the top of his workspace with a green tent; purchased, it seems, from the Army Surplus store around the corner.

He was obviously going to spend the night and challenge anyone who would dare try to "clean up" his workspace. Plans were revamped to avoid that side of the hallway in The Land of Assistant Whatevers during the client tour.

It was Friday morning and before I even settled in at my cubicle, I could smell the panic. The client had called and would be arriving early and wanted to take the tour before the formal Presentation, and had cut short the total time they would spend with us; largely because they had a change of flight plans and would be heading home to Tokyo earlier than expected. Since we were the last of the presenters, it seemed like the whole thing was doomed. Everyone was running around like beheaded fowl. The two Babes who would be assisting in the in-house lunch for the Presentation were busy calling the downtown deli from which we ordered every in-house lunch to send the sandwich-platters over at 11:00 a.m. rather than 11:45 a.m., and doing some last minute prepping of their own. Short, low-cut, tight dress, check. High heels, check. Big hair and lip gloss, check, check.

Now I only mention what we were serving because one of the other major agencies, who presented two days earlier had arranged for lunch at *YAMASHIRO'S* which in the '80s was a well-known and very "authentic" Japanese restaurant in the Hollywood hills, complete with soothing gardens and koi ponds and lovely Geishas tending to your every need. And after their presentation, the whole group was driven there in black stretch limos, and then came back and took a tour of their no-doubt impressive offices. Both of the other agencies had their business cards translated into Japanese...though why they thought that made any sense at all was completely beside the point. They even took lessons on how to bow and properly present a business card, which is a ritual of the utmost skill. Bow too shallow...not good, present your card too soon or too late ... perilous.

Furthermore, one of the other agencies had sent out their leave-behinds, which is the book that contains everything that will be shown to them in the presentation, and had them bound in raw silk fabric, and coupled that with a very expensive sterling silver pen with which to take notes, a gift to each member of the potential new client team. Our books had been copied in-house, and bound at the local Kinko's in basic black pseudo-leather. I had ordered our pens from the office supply book...nice, but not too fancy, a step up from a BIC. We were after all, the dark horse in this race and none of TPTB wanted to break the bank trying to get a client that was such a long shot.

The client arrived. Lots of firm handshaking and introductions in the Reception area under the watchful eye of our Receptionist, who had been a model in her previous life, as well as the ex-wife of a well-known NFL player, and who was, at that time, probably the only African-American Adland receptionist on Wilshire Blvd. (Think Whitney Houston in her prime.)

One of the Presentation Babes, a striking redhead, with large gray-green eyes, and a impressive figure barely contained in a Kelly-green dress, which was this agency's corporate color, came out to let the Presentation Team know the Conference Room was ready, and led the way in her best "Vanna White" impersonation. They were shown to their seats and our team started handing out their business cards, with absolutely no ceremony. The client remained on their feet.

"We take tour, first, yes?"

Lots of nodding ensued on both sides of the table.

"Oh, yes, sure. Why not?"

And then Fate stepped in. Instead of turning towards "Vanna" and heading left, the client turned right and down the corridor towards the Creative Department and The

Land of Assistant Whatevers. They were busy chatting amongst themselves in Japanese, and nodding politely, as our team swept up the rear.

But before TPTB could head them off, they stopped at Moe's cubicle. The tent top was gone, the paper piles were gone. The client stuck their heads in at first, then stepped in and one by one started to speak in rapid-fire Japanese, and then broke out into laughter which erupted into loud approving "Aaahs" and "Ooohs."

No, Moe had not been fired. And his workstation had not been ambushed. Neither had he taken down any of the pictures. In fact, Moe was sitting in his workstation at his drafting table, drawing. He had taken a shower…probably at the gym up the street, had on a clean shirt and shoes (!), his hair was neatly pulled back and he had even trimmed his beard, if only a little.

What he had done was pure genius, for covering every inch of his walls was brown wrapping paper, stenciled with the words "X-RATED."

The client spent about 30 minutes peeking under the paper. And Moe showed them his drawings of his favorite motorcycles, *Harley-Davidson, Indian Chiefs,* and *Triumph* among others, and how happy he was they had come to visit us.

Back in the conference room, at the end of the presentation, the client did what I found out later they had not done in any of the other meetings, they stood up and applauded! They stayed for the deli-lunch and had seconds of the potato salad and kosher pickles; they shook hands with the Gents and hugged the Babes. They went home to Tokyo and on Monday morning we had ourselves a motorcycle account!

And Moe … well, he moved out of his cubicle in The Land of Assistant Whatevers and up the hall into a small inside office within yelling distance of the Executive VP, Creative Director. He still faunched and bellowed at everyone who annoyed him and did work on the New Business as was, I suspect, his plan all along. Before I left this agency for another job in Adland, I went to see him and he told me, as only Moe could, to "Fuck you and Good Luck!"

Somewhere along the way between this final farewell and my time at HIP, Inc., he had met and wisely married a kind, funny, gentle and talented Babe, who somehow, someway, changed him into an equally kind, funny, gentle (and still talented) Gent. He was no longer Angry Moe.

But that's a story for another day...

Chapter 10

SHE-BABE OF ADLAND

For your listening pleasure: *"Simply Irresistible"* - *Robert Palmer*

Quote for the day: *"Yeah, well with one of these, I can get ten of those."*

When I was a kid, my mother and father would take me to the drive-in movie; a double feature, during which time by the second movie, they were sure I would fall asleep, so ratings (if there were any then,) be damned.

Usually, they were science-fiction extravaganzas, like *Godzilla*, or *Godzilla vs. Mothra*, or *Godzilla Battles King Kong*, *Invaders from Mars*, *Attack of the Mole People*, *Frankenstein Meets the Wolf Man* ... you get my drift. Good old-fashioned, harmless horror and mayhem. Actually, I really liked these movies, and it was my parents who usually fell asleep, and I who got an eyeful.

And then one night, when I was 10 years old, I saw a movie and realized what I wanted to be when I grew up: *"She Who Must Be Obeyed."* A fine little Hammer Studios film, circa 1965; starring that BABE to whom most all Babes stand in awe ... Ursula Andress. Who could forget her in *Dr. No*, or *What's New Pussycat*, or even her two-part appearance on *The Love Boat*? She was so incredibly beautiful, and in this movie, *She*, incredibly powerful!

Never mind that I would (A) never be that bodacious, (B) never command that kind of envy, and (C) would always be the one who cleaned up the wreckage these types of women create just by existing in a world where power either has a dick or knows how to make it stand at attention and beg for more.

At one time there were two such powerful women on staff. One was in Creative and one worked in Media. Sadly, when all was said and done, both fell from grace and were never heard from again ... in Adland anyway.

This story focuses on Jayne, Executive VP, Media Director, a Lauren Bacall-type blonde, whose shoulders did not need the padding that was so popular in '80s fashion. She had a trim waist and legs that went on for days. She accentuated her already tall and heroic figure with heels as high as she could walk in and still stride confidently down the hall to conference rooms, or to Mr. Hamilton's office. She never went to any other place in the agency. If someone from the Account Group wanted to take a meeting, or if a question from Finance or HR came up that required her in-person attention, then that person, no matter their title, had just better haul their ass down to see her in her office, or as we called it, The Palace.

Now you may wonder with everything I have said so far, exactly how a female rose to such a position of power in Adland, and most especially, HIP, Inc.? Simply put, she was Mathilde C. Weil, Helen Resor and Mary Wells all rolled into one; as driven, talented, brazen and brash as any Gent or any of TPTB. She was the little girl growing up who, as the joke goes when a boy pointed to his penis with pride and is quickly shot down because she points to her female area, and retorts, "Yeah, well with one of these, I can get ten of those!"

Jayne started her career as an Assistant Whatever Babe, in a small in-house agency for a well-known stereo chain. At eighteen, she was stunning and smart ... smart enough to know that working in the accounting pit (a sea of blonde, stacked and barely-legal-aged Babes) at this little company could lead to great things. She showed the company owners not only how to save money on everything from their product supplier contracts, but how to barter in electronic goods, and sometimes coke, rather than cash, for radio air time and newspaper space. She was one of the first to demonstrate the benefit of sponsoring the latest rock concert and was front and center for car wash/wet t-shirt events at the company's flagship store on Sunset Blvd., across the street from the then-famous Tower Records, featuring the latest up and coming music celebrity.

She moved on from there to a movie studio and finagled what others might have seen as a step back to another Assistant Babe assignment in their emerging video library division. By age 28, she was in partnership owning one of the first Blockbuster franchises. She paid cash for a condo in Century City and ventured into buying, rehabbing and selling small rentals in "transition" neighborhoods on the Westside. She had fingers in pies ranging from art to music, real estate to all forms of media. And she had her eye on only one thing, a position with HIP, Inc. as their Maven of Media ... a job which she was not completely qualified for, having never actually worked in Adland before. But that's where a certain member of TPTB came in.

"How in Hell did she get this job anyway? That's what I want to know."

"Burt (apparently in line for the job) was way more qualified, and now he's out on his ass."

"Yeah, that really blows. You work like a dog, and then, screw you!"

"I'll bet she got hers the 'old-fashioned way' ..."

"No doubt about that ... but who 'sponsored' her?"

"And who's going to work for her? I hear she's a real bitch."

All the Babes (and a few of the Gents) in Adland were none too pleased.

Naturally, at first, all fingers pointed to Mr.. Hamilton, but upon further subtle inquiries, he was not the one who made this play.

Mr. Ingersoll had just "resigned" a Creative Babe who, they say, ran afoul of the client once too often and we all know where that leads ... the unemployment line. What amazes me, in hindsight, is that this Babe was very talented and had done great work for her clients, and had she been M-A-L-E, her take-no-prisoners attitude would have been praised rather than perceived as the "B" (not BABE) word. (I am happy to say, however, that that particular woman ended up being very happy and successful in both her own business and her personal life outside of Adland ... yes, it is possible to have a real life after death!)

It might have been Mr. Pride, but no one had the guts to venture down this path.

So, wherever the job offering sprang from, Human Remains was busy making ready for her first day.

"She has a few requests for her office ... here's the list. I'm sure you will accommodate her."

(But of course. That is what I do after all, give people, the ones that have the power anyway, what they want when they want it and figure out a way to ease the pain of a "No" or a "Maybe," which will probably turn into a "No," to everyone else.)

On Monday, she would be moving into the corner office formerly occupied by the previous VP, Media Director. Or so I was told. Wrong.

She apparently came in over the weekend, and moved into the office next door, also a corner, due to the building's odd structure, and had re-arranged all the remaining furniture to better suit the Feng Shui. There was a pile of boxes, furniture and other odd 'n ends in the office she did not take and her new Assistant ... a Babe no one knew, delivered a note to me with revisions to the note HR had given me:

> *Hi, there ~* (What, am I now a destination?)
> *Hope you don't mind about the swap, but I just didn't really feel quite at home in that office.* (How would you know ... you spent 5 minutes in it!) *I've kept the desk for now, but all the other furniture simply will not do. Here is what I want:*
> 1. *A new sofa, which will be delivered here tomorrow. I've enclosed the bill.* (It's leather, naturally, a large corner unit, well above the price point I have in my budget, and it's in a color called "Urban Blush.")

2. Two guest chairs, which will be delivered tomorrow as well. I've enclosed that bill. (Double scraped wool, in a color called "Warm.")

3. I'm having my own desk brought in, along with a side table, a coffee table and a rug. Here is the bill for the delivery charge. Please be sure to tip the driver and his helper ... they work for me all the time. (Then, why, pray tell, are you not tipping them? And do they have insurance to cover HIP, Inc. in case they get injured?)

4. I want a large plant. It's called a "Finger Cactus" (I'll just bet it is ...), *but I want a very specific shape, so just have your plant service bring in 3 or 4 for me to choose from. I'd like it in place by Friday, please.* (Well, she does have manners.)

5. Please arrange to have one wall (I've marked it) painted. Here is the PANTONE chip. (A lovely shade of grey ... I was beginning to like her ... or at least her taste.) *I'd like to see this done over this next weekend. (*But of course you would.)

6. A desk chair, from my home, which will be delivered on Friday. I've included the delivery ticket. (This Babe really did have taste ... Eames Aluminum Group hi-back in black leather ... way over the price point.)

7. I'd like to have a weekly delivery of a single flower for my desk. It doesn't matter what type, so long as it's Violet. (Obviously, she knew the corporate color here at HIP, Inc. is purple. We chose this color because P-B Industries uses this color, which they label "amatory," in every shade for their S-E-X products.)

Thnx.

J.

"She has lovely penmanship ... so rare these days." The Sphinx was in fine form when I showed her the note.

"That's it? That's all you have to say about this?"

She simply smiled and we left it at that.

I spent that week, greeting (and tipping) all the delivery people (the plant people had to make two trips since the first offering was rebuffed) and waited that Saturday for the painters to finish, making doubly sure the color, when dried, was a perfect match for the swatch.

It was a beautiful office; comfortable and welcoming, but at the same time, there was an undercurrent that the woman who sat in it was no pushover.

The Babes found out that her Assistant Babe was named Carole, and she was She-Babe's Personal Assistant, also an Adland virgin. She was actually more of a "vintage" Babe than most, and had her own company called 'Need Notary, Will Travel." Apparently, this is how she first met Jayne. Her much younger, longtime boyfriend was a dude who, in certain celebrity circles, was a well-known and reliable Psychic Adviser, and Jayne depended on his services as well. Please allow me to offer this praise ... Carole was without doubt one of the sweetest and kindest women I ever had the pleasure to know. This Babe always, always looked at the good side of things, reached out to the best in a person and was incredibly patient when it came to handling the stream-of-consciousness requests from her Boss-Lady Babe.

"Carole, I need you to **cancel** my 10 o'clock with Mr.. Hamilton. Please tell him I'm available at 3 if that works, and get Smith from The Times on the line? Also, tell Daphne I'll be late for my appointment, but I **will** be there, so don't even think about canceling. And bring me my lunch at 11:00 ... I'll take the Chicken Salad from Chin Chin's, with two dressings, on the side. Make **sure** they bring chopsticks. And is that spreadsheet I asked for ready yet? I'm going to twist those numbers around Smith's neck so hard, he's going to beg to pay **us** for the space in his upcoming special edition. Special edition, my ass ... BLAH, BLAH ... BLAH, BLAH, BLAH."

"Sure, Jayne ... no worries."

Thanks, in part, to the planning and buying skills of She-Babe's growing staff of females ... some of whom came from the current stable of talented Babes, and some from other agencies, where the exploits of She-Babe were becoming legend ... HIP, Inc.'s bottom line was improving. The clients were happy, TPTB were happy, no one more so than JP, whom it turned out was the "sponsor" who put in a good word for She-Babe. She had done so well, that Jayne was being recognized at a national media forum that weekend in NYC held in conjunction with the annual Cleo Awards celebrated that year at the Waldorf-Astoria. The Ramrod Account Team was also going. What should have been a long weekend, turned into a week, and no one knew where she was, and why she hadn't come back with the rest of the group.

You can imagine my shock then, when arriving early the following Monday morning not only to find The Palace had been ransacked, but that She-Babe was no more.

Conference Room Alpha was filling up with people and the usual morning banter ...

"The way I heard it was, she put in for a few days of R & R in the Bahamas tacked on to the end of that big media conference in NY. If she hadn't had that gastrointestinal problem and wound up in the hospital, she would have come back and resigned anyway."

"So he actually saw her at the resort sitting with Mr. Young?"

"Yeah, and Mr.. Winston was there too. She was holding court, all right ... poolside – smoking, drinking, laughing and flirting – you know, the way she did with all TPTB and the reps."

"Serves her right."

"Hey, maybe Burt will come back? I miss him!"

"Who in their right mind would want to come back here?"

"What? It's not so bad here ... we're a country club compared to other shops."

And so the conversations went back and forth that Jayne was asked to resign after Mr. Hamilton caught her with the enemy in a compromising situation. That he was also in a compromising situation, away from home, with the newest and oh, so, sponsorable Babe ... well, that's just Adland for you.

But that's a story for another day ....

Chapter 11

ALL THAT ASIDE

For your listening pleasure: *"Don't Worry Be Happy"* - *Bobby McFerrin*

Quote for the day: *"I didn't sleep my way into this job ... my mother did that for me!"*

What follows is a collection of musings, information, facts, observations, and suppositions that are in no particular order or level of importance and yet, may serve to provide further insights into the world of Adland.

If the Furniture Could Talk

Not everyone in Adland wants a hot tub, but everyone in Adland does want a sofa. Somehow this innocuous item of furniture defines your status in any office, but most particularly in a Creative office. If you are low man (or Babe) on the totem pole, you might get a one- or two-piece sectional in a canvas material from *IKEA*, or you might have to settle for a bean bag chair which you buy yourself, bring in and find a way to expense it.

If you have a bit of tenure under your belt and have actually produced an ad that was published or a commercial that was even considered by the client, then you might qualify for a real loveseat in a real fabric, chosen from a limited range of swatches, in sturdy fabrics that will go in anyone's office. (Translation, the office down the hall of the guy who replaces you when you strike out on the next campaign, which everyone inevitably does sooner or later.) Finally, after a long time, when you have several ads in your portfolio, and rumors are rampant that you are being wooed by the hot new agency down the road, you can confidently negotiate three things: a window office, more money, and a new leather sofa.

When Words Fail Me

Now mind you, every writer has fleeting moments of "writer's block," but when your entire career depends on your ability to spew forth words, words, words and ideas, ideas, ideas ... and all you got is nothing, nothing nothing ... you are in deep shit, my friend.

Early in my Adland career, I met a successful copywriter who told me he didn't believe it was a real issue. "I come in, get the assignment and write and then I go home and don't think about it. And the following week or month, I do the same thing ... it's a skill, not a gift. I work at my craft and I don't assign any hocus-pocus to it. It's a job."

The 15% Solution

Strictly speaking, Media is an odd component of the Adland formula. Media companies give agencies a discounted, or net, price for their services, and the agency charges the client a different amount, or the gross amount. This difference between net and gross is traditionally 15% and if you have large clients who spend millions, this amount affords the agency a solid income. These contracts are on a commission bases, and this commission is supposed to cover all the costs of producing an ad and, hopefully, allow for a decent profit.

Contracts on a fee basis are when a client, usually smaller ones, pay a negotiated price for the production of their ads, and then the net costs (or near net costs) are passed on.

The first sign of trouble in this arena came when one of our larger clients asked us ..."Hey, how about I pay you, say ... 12% this year?"

"How about if I slit my wrists?"

"How about my wife (partner, boyfriend, girlfriend, bookie, dealer, mistress ...) leaves me because I can't pay for their whatevers (house, car, credit cards, facelift, drugs, life coach ...)?"

"How about I fire all the really good staffers (writers, art directors, account reps) and hire the has-beens, or the wannabes, so I can afford to keep you as my client, thereby not losing face in Adland?"

And yet, don't you know, we said ... fine ... sure ... no problem ... 12%? Sounds like a plan ... now would you mind signing an extension to our current agreement ... say for another 5 years? And that is partly why HIP, Inc. now has an agreement for 8% ... as do many other shops in Adland.

The Goose that Laid the Golden Graft

For the longest time, graft was flowing through our Media Department like grease through a duck. What is graft, you ask? Well this is another odd component in the Adland formula of compensation ... one that rarely gets the attention it deserves, and thank goodness for that because all through the '80s this was one of the things that made life in Adland worthwhile. (I won't go into how this "tragically" changed in the decade that followed ... something about a Gent, on the client side of all places, who wrote a book, and blew the cover off all those gifts of cash, trips, cars, coke, clothes, concert tickets, etc., right on down to the little caps, t-shirts, and bags that were festooned with the name of a client or their product. Even RAMROD caps were a thing of the past and anyone who had one coveted them with pride. Graft that could boost your private bottom line was now cuckolded into a $25 or less harness from which the only escape was outside the boundaries of HIP, Inc., or any other agency. Sniff ... tear ... sniff ... tear ...)

What is My Talent Worth?

Adland can be a place ripe with generosity. I don't mean the salaries ... because as any Babe and low-level Gent or Tot, male and female, will tell you, they suck. No. Generous totally depends on how well connected you are. For example, if you are a creative genius, or one of TPTB, or, however distant, related to TPTB, or the client, or sometimes, but not a given, to the creative genius, unless he or she happens to be one of TPTB, and so on, then the matter of your worth will be higher or lower based on this rather than ... say ... talent?

What talent you bring to the table can be measured in many ways because worth and talent are really two different things in Adland and especially at HIP, Inc. You may be worth quite a lot, with your Ivy League Master's Degree in Marketing, and all the ripe-with-compliments letters from your professors and other head honchos from Adland sites where you interned rather than skiing in Gstaad or sunning in Ibiza, but because the nephew of your client's first-of-three ex-wives, to whom substantial alimony is still being paid, has more value, sadly, but not inexplicably, your well-won, impressive background will be trumped in a New York minute, in favor of someone with no perceptible skills, or aspiration, and who may not be that literate or even able to articulate a complete and grammatically correct sentence.

And so the 1978 bumper sticker rings as true today here in Adland as it did on those VW micro-buses on their way to the next open air rock festival: "Ass, Gas or Grass, Nobody Rides for Free!"

Drugs? Just Say Yes!
Overheard at an agency cocktail party: "I didn't sleep my way into this job ... my mother did that for me!"

Revelations like this one could sure bring a Babe, or a Gent for that matter, down. Which is why so many in Adland turn to drugs! Oh sure, everyone knows the recreational joint or the twice weekly three-drink minimum lunch is hardly going to land you broke, dirty, homeless, jobless, lying in an alley somewhere or at the freeway carrying one of those handwritten signs ..." WILL WRITE ADS FOR FOOD" ... but this may happen to you if you think all the rules of engagement do not apply to you.

Allow me to expound on this point. In Adland, where the pressure is constant, the pay is usually low, unless as mentioned you are A) Connected, B) Brilliant, or C) Brilliant and Connected to either the client or one of TPTB. Your job security rises and falls on how solid this connection is and so you will do just about anything – legality and morality are not at play herein – to maintain this. The only exception I ever knew about, but could never do anything about is the one person who is untouchable in any agency ... the Dude or the Babe who supplies the drugs.

Now in Adland, and blessedly so, tequila, vodka, beer, wine, champagne, etc., especially during lunch, in a meeting, a company-wide party or celebration of a new client, is perfectly acceptable. In fact, it's a given that at some point in your career, you will get shit-faced and do something or say something embarrassing or foolish, or even nearly career-ending; however, you will probably be doing this when everyone else is in a similar state, so by the time said everyone sobers, up, all is forgiven and forgotten ... unless you have a Polaroid.

You remember Claire ... of course you do. She parlayed her little dossier of pictorial interest into a substantial raise ('bout time!) a larger office with the standard leather sofa, a better title and once she had accomplished all that was offered, an even better gig at one of HIP, Inc.'s fiercest competitors, the aforementioned YS&W (Young, Smart and With-it,) and was in the process of pitching the account she had been handling for years at HIP, Inc. This turned into a very protracted, bitter, full of name-calling, backbiting, hair-pulling – and this was only our internal side of it – campaign competition that ever graced the pages of *Adweek* and *Ad Age*. It may have made Page Six but then who cared; we were West Coast Adland and didn't give a damn about what our East Coast brethren thought.

So with tensions flying high ... enter Raphael, full-time janitor, part-time dealer. A polite young man who was supplying just about every level of personnel in HIP, Inc., with their drug of choice ... Cocaine, Pot, Pills, possibly H, whatever and who cares, as long as you showed up for your meetings, kowtowed to the clients as appropriate, wrote your copy, directed your art, and produced your commercial brilliantly, made sure the Media paper was pushed and the minutes or inches were well-negotiated, and you kept your Traffic and Production schedules on their mark.

I'm guessing he was on speed-dial, too, for lots of people in and out of Adland, which could explain how no matter that he was lousy at his job ... "Can someone please get my trash can emptied!!! It's only been a fucking week ..." he still had it.

It was really quite a simple set-up. Kind of like ordering Chinese take-out ... one from Column A, two from Column B. You dialed a number (which was changed frequently) left a message about playing Pool (coke) Baseball (pot), Chess (pills) or Football (H) and then checked under your new trash liner to receive your order and leave your payment. Anyone who might intercept the message would think you were placing a bet with a bookie or really wanted to set up a game of pool ... "Yeah, this is #6, I'd like to know if you can set up a game of 8-ball tomorrow night?" ... like that was legal, but not as bad as scoring. If the number changed, no problem, you'd find it written somewhere on your whiteboard with a red (coke,) green (pot,) pink (pills,) or purple (H) marker.

If you took the time and paid attention, you knew who was doing what and how often. Useful information which I never had to parlay to my advantage, because everyone probably thought I was on drugs ... or should be ... Thorazine comes to mind ...

"No, it doesn't."

"Yes, it does."

Well, you get the picture.

Actually, my experience being pharmaceutically straight jacketed in detox, long considered and finally absolutely needed after a terrible family tragedy, was the first time I was able to really relax ... hard to worry about deadlines, or giving orders or making plans when you can barely put a cohesive sentence together. Anyway, apparently, in spite of my penchant for a potent cocktail now and then, I am not an "alcoholic." I just like to drink when I am stressed, and since being TOM, I am stressed more than most by all the goings on in Adland.

So, after three days in lock-down, they sized me up and kicked me out as they wanted to make room for someone who was actually ill, and I spent the remainder of that 6-week "vacation" traversing the planet, visiting Stonehenge, a short stay at Findhorn, in honor of one of my favorite films, *My Dinner With Andre*, two nights in Sedona, where I did see what I believe to be a UFO, and finally a week of absolute bliss at Two-Bunch Palms, taking in their world-famous waters and mud baths, never mind that last-minute dash to Lourdes ... just in case.

Wiser, and cheaper to eat healthy, run daily along the beach, pray, laugh, and not take it all so seriously. After all, "It's a business. It ain't art." It's just Adland ...

The Great Escape
I'm sure there are as yet unidentified vortexes that lie just

outside and down the street from most Adland sites. Sedona-esque places dismayed and depressed agency folk fall into and are usually never heard from again, when they have, a) lost an account, b) lost a promotion, and as a result of said "a" or "b," c) lost their beloved office with its soft, plump, soothing, luscious leather, highly coveted – as in "I'd sell my first born for a *Roche Bobois*" – sofa.

It is a well-known but little discussed fact that people in Adland have been known to simply vanish during lunch, while stepping out for a morning or afternoon break, after work, or on the weekend, or just about anytime these *Twilight Zone*-ish incidences occur. Naturally, they "say," "Oh, I'll be right back," or "Just heading out for a smoke," or "Leaving early, need time to re-group," but really they fall into a black hole and in a few days their last check is sent to them, with a Human Remains note that admonishes in pages and pages of CYA legalese that they never, ever, ever return to this little slice of Adland. Unless, like Elliott Monroe, you are plucked back into this time-space continuum because, a) the client likes you, b) you have dirt on either the agency or the client, or both, or c) all of the above.

Since Adland is one of the most incestuous industries on the face of Mother Earth, the other being the "entertainment" biz (within which Adland falls, but only in the minds of the completely confused), and possibly law firms, said MIA personnel will eventually show up in another quadrant of Adland, usually on a competing account, with an increase in salary, a better office and a softer, plumper, more soothing and even more luscious "Yes, I love the smell of leather, Babe!" – sofa.

Epilogue

*L*ooking back on it all, I wouldn't trade one moment of my "career" in Adland for anything. I learned a lot. I think others learned from me. And I have only the utmost respect for the real Gents and Babes I had the privilege and the pride to work for and with. Many are now out of the biz, and have moved on to their real lives ... not the make-believe world of Adland. I hope they enjoy their "memories" as much as I.

Of course, there are those stories for another day...

Here are three that come to mind:

~ "Who's that guy?"

"Well, I hope you know; he works for you."

"I never saw him before ... when did he get here?"

"About a month ago ... he has an office on the 7th floor ... never mind, I'm calling HR."

~ "I counted twice. We're short three cameras."

"Well, I told you it was a bad idea to leave disposable cameras on the tables at the Annual Staff-Only Company Picnic."

"I'll send out a memo ...."

"Don't bother ... just pray they never surface."

~ "I have a confession to make...you know that Ming vase that was "stolen" from the Christmas Party venue?

"Yes, I'm really upset ... they called the police and reported it ... I just hope I get my hands on the employee first! My good standing at the club is on the line here."

"Well, reach out and touch someone, sir ... I'm your Babe!"

113

Glossary

ADLAND: An advertising agency, or the entire advertising industry.

ACCOUNT: A client's business and how it's handled in Adland.

AD: Short for an advertisement or the word "advertising."

AGENCY: Short for an ad agency.

ASSISTANT WHATEVERS: Low-level writers, art directors, account coordinators, who are one step above TOTS.

BABE: A woman who works in Adland. (Note: All Babes are women, but not all women are Babes.)

HONORARY-BABE: A man who works in Adland, deemed worthy of being called a BABE.

WANNA-BE-BABE: A woman who works in Adland, but not deemed worthy of being called a BABE.

BOSS: See GENT.

CLIENT: A firm or individual that hires an ad agency.

CRICKETS: "chirp, chirp, chirp," Nothing is happening or being said. (See SILENCE.)

DILDO: If you have to ask what this S-E-X toy is for, don't buy one!

DOMINATRIX: A woman who inflicts pain and humiliation on a man for money. (See WIFE.)

"EST": Erhard Seminars Training; part of the "human potential movement" from 1971-1984.

FILL-IN-BABE: Also called a FLOATER.

FREDDIE GIRLS: Assistants to Mr. Ingersoll.

GENT: A man who works in Adland. Might be called a DUDE. Or might be your BOSS.

HARMONY SPRINGS: Rehab facility in the Malibu mountains; Elliott Monroe's second home away from home.

HIP, INC.: The ad agency, "Hamilton, Ingersoll & Pride, Inc."

ILLEGALLY BLONDE: A BABE who has made her mark in Adland, and is moving up the ladder.

JOLT: Before there was RED BULL, there was Jolt.

LOTF: Lord of the Flies; Quentin, Copywriter on the Ramrod Account.

M-A-L-E: The strictly heterosexual, non-female of the species.

MENTAL HEALTH DAY: You're not "sick" exactly; you just need a respite from Adland.

MISTRESS: A woman who wants to be a WIFE. (See YOU KNOW WHO.)

OSS/OSP: Office Services Specialist, Office Services Professional

PBI: Prichard-Bailey Industries, largest client for HIP, Inc.

PITCH: The "Dog and Pony Show" to illustrate to your client, or potential client what you can do to promote their product or service. Also called a PRESENTATION.

PLAYERS: Anyone willing to enter into the game that is Adland.

REPS: Representatives of media outlets who want your ads to run on, or appear in the magazines, newspapers, or TV shows they have as clients. In the '80s most REPS were young men because most Adland MEDIA jobs were held by women ... you get the picture.

REVIEW: Often an exercise in futility, this is where the agency has to prove to the client they are worthy of keeping the business.

S-E-X: Male, female, intercourse or whatever "it" is.

SILENCE: Not always golden, especially if it's a client reaction to your PITCH. (See Crickets.)

THE SPHINX: Frances, HIP, Inc.'s Receptionist

TPTB: The Powers That Be; these are the head honchos who run an agency.

TOM: The Office Mom

TOT: Someone who is just starting out in Adland, usually as a secretary or a clerk, or a low-level ASSISTANT WHATEVER.

WIFE: A woman who inflicts pain and humiliation on a man for money (see DOMINATRIX)

YOU KNOW WHO: (See Mistress.)

YS&W: Young, Sellers & Winston; aka Young, Smart & With-it; chief competition of HIP, Inc.

Thnx

A sincere thank you to all the unnamed and completely anonymous men, women, gender-fluid individuals, clients, vendors, products, law enforcement agencies, law firms, rehab facilities, "personal services" workers, and animals who were in no way meant to be hurt during the writing of this book. All the stories, while each having, perhaps, a miniscule element of truth, are absolutely, 100% a product of this writer's vivid imagination. But just so you know, the "unedited" version, safely tucked away with specific instructions, is to be published upon my untimely demise, and any news stories that I have "committed suicide" or was "abducted by aliens" are not to be taken seriously! (And of course there are those Polaroids. But that's a story for another day ...)

- TOM

Thank you for reading.
Please review this book. Reviews help others find Absolutely Amazing eBooks and inspire us to keep providing these marvelous tales.

If you would like to be put on our email list to receive updates on new releases, contests, and promotions, please go to AbsolutelyAmazingEbooks.com and sign up.

About the Author

Monica De Vargas, in her debut novel, *The Typing Room*, explored an entirely different approach to the world of Alzheimer's patients and the nearly 16-million family caregivers in the United States whose lives are profoundly affected by this disease.

In this novel she writes about the advertising world that she knows so well. Monica has worked for some of the largest ad agencies in Los Angeles as a self-described "Office Mom." After a thirty-year career, she and her husband relocated from Venice Beach to a farm in rural Oklahoma. They now live in Tulsa, with their three canine companions.

The New
Atlantian Library

NewAtlantianLibrary.com
or AbsolutelyAmazingeBooks.com
or AA-eBooks.com

www.ingramcontent.com/pod-product-compliance
Lightning Source LLC
Chambersburg PA
CBHW050411030726
47503CB00006B/2137